ESCAPE!

by

R.L. Leader

First published 1989
Second edition 2017

ISBN: 978-1568716428

Published by
Targum Publishers
Shlomo ben Yosef 131a/1
Jerusalem 93805
editor@targumpublishers.com

In loving memory of
Albert M. Sharon, *z"l*

...very pleasant hast thou been to me;
Wonderful was thy love for me....
How are the mighty fallen....
II Samuel 1:26-27

And in memory of my beloved brother,
Eugene Leader, *z"l*

May their memory forever be a blessing.

SPRING 1844

Chapter 1

THE FIRE ILLUMINATED the moonless night, casting eerie, flickering shadows. Reuven stretched and shifted on the rutted ground and pulled his tattered blanket tighter around him. He gazed at the ten exhausted youths curled into shivering balls around the campfire. Spring was late in coming this year, and the night was cold.

He edged closer to his friend, his ears straining. All he could hear were the sounds of the night and Archik's even breathing. Archik did not stir. Was he really asleep or was it just another one of his pranks? Reuven wanted to reach out and touch him, whisper his name, but he dared not make a sound. He laid his head on the wet earth, and the thought of their escape taunted him.

Reuven had so wanted to include the others in their scheme, but Archik was adamant. "There isn't a chance in the world for ten conscripts to get away," he had explained. There was no arguing with his friend's logic. Still, the thought of leaving the children, many of them conscripted into the Czar's brutal army at the age of nine or ten, troubled his conscience.

Reuven twisted and turned on the muddy ground, wondering whether he had been misled by his mischievous friend. Perhaps the escape plan he'd concocted had been no more than a fantasy, a way to while away the hours. Then again, Archik was only fourteen, one year younger than Reuven, and perhaps sleep had simply overtaken him. The long march had been brutal, the last week torturous. They had slogged through mile after mile of thick mud. Now, still over a hundred miles from their destination, the army base in Kalinin, Corporal Kolchak had grudgingly surrendered to the inevitable. Not even his curses and whip could budge the horses. The wagon carrying soldiers and supplies remained mired in the muddy earth and the conscripts dropped where they stood, too numb to care.

Again Reuven squinted at his friend in the flickering light. He wanted to shout, "Wake up, wake up! We're losing our chance for freedom!" But all he did was stare at Archik's back in growing despair.

Reuven closed his eyes and the memory of their first meeting came back to him. He had been resting in his freezing barracks one evening when eleven half-starved new conscripts had stumbled into the room, their lips purple, their eyes glazed. As he looked at their emaciated faces, Reuven vividly remembered his own first days as a conscript. Like so many other unfortunates, he'd been nabbed by "*khappers*," men hired by desperate village councils to fill the Czar's unyielding quota of Jews. The boys were to undergo six years in a "canton," a brutal army camp designed to break their spirits and force them to accept baptism. Those who lived through the horrors of the cantons were then placed in the army for twenty-five years.

Reuven had survived those first terrifying months, and survived them as a Jew. Now it was his job to comfort the new arrivals.

One paper-thin boy swaggered toward him, his pale blue eyes staring out of his hunger-pinched face, his bony hand extended.

"My name is Aharon Leib Gottlieb, but my friends call me Archik."

Startled by the boy's cheeky tone, Reuven returned the lad's grin in spite of himself. It felt good to smile again. "I'm Reuven Fenster."

"And what do your friends call you?" the lad teased with a good-natured smile.

"I guess you can call me Reuven."

Unexpectedly they had become friends, despite Shmulik Marmelstein's warning to be wary of the prankster with the impish smile. The other conscripts had also muttered their disapproval of Archik, though their eyes danced with admiration for him. There was no doubt that his antics often bordered on the irresponsible and even on the dangerous. On occasion Reuven had tried to temper his new friend's impetuousness, such as when Archik picked a fight with a soldier who spat and cursed whenever a conscript walked by. Still, he couldn't help but marvel at Archik's spunk, evidenced only too frequently by a black eye and bloodied nose, which he wore as a badge of defiance. Perhaps it was Archik's high spirits that drew Reuven to the new boy. Somehow the lad's buoyant personality eased the pain of his separation from home and family.

If it was Archik who kept the barracks in an uproar with his exploits, it was Reuven, soft-spoken and meek, who strengthened the conscripts' waning faith. He knew how important it was to bolster their resolve to resist their tormentors.

"They can torture our bodies, but they can never destroy our *neshamos*!" he told them with fervor. "The only way we can defeat them is through our *tefillos*, our learning, and our faith. These are our weapons."

Reuven davened with the boys and reviewed the blessings recited before and after meals. He also taught them the *halachos* of Shabbos, showing them how some forms of *melachah* could be avoided. And he spoke to them of *mesiras nefesh*, of sacrifice, and of the reward that awaited them in the World to Come. Archik, Reuven noticed with concern, often stayed away from those clandestine classes, spending his few free hours sitting moodily on the thin pallet that served as his bed.

In a matter of months, under the relatively humane treatment of the base commander, Lieutenant Suslovsky, Aharon Leib Gottlieb changed from an undernourished waif into a strikingly handsome lad. His shaved head began sprouting wisps of fair hair, his gaunt face filled out, and freckles butterflied across his turned-up nose and onto his cheeks.

Archik soon revealed an uncanny ability to exploit every opportunity for his own benefit. When he was named Lieutenant Suslovsky's personal attendant, it took him almost no time to "liberate" the officer's military map. The thief was never apprehended, and the lieutenant never dreamed that a pathetic cantonist could be so impudent.

Archik kept the precious map of Russia well hidden. Only when the other boys were fast asleep would he carefully unfold it and draw up possible escape routes. Archik soon became obsessed with his dreams of freedom, and when he overheard the officers discuss the conscripts' transfer west to the camp in Kalinin, he did not rest until he had worked out a plan.

Reuven tried to dissuade him, pointing to the danger and futility of the scheme. "No cantonist has ever escaped from an army base," Reuven argued.

"Do you want to remain a slave for the rest of your life?" Archik shot back. "You keep talking about Hashem and how He will help us. Well, all I know is that if Hashem sends us an opportunity, we are obligated to grab it!"

Reuven's resistance crumbled as his gnawing, everpresent homesickness grew stronger. Just when he had finally forbidden himself the luxury of dwelling upon a past that he could never relive, he found himself thinking of his parents, his *shtetl*, the life he had loved. In the end, he'd agreed. Perhaps, he thought to himself, their mad plan might work. Perhaps he would one day be reunited with his family. Now, he wondered: Was it to end here, on this cold ground, on this journey to Kalinin?

"Reuven! Reuven!"

Reuven opened his eyes. Squatting at his side was Archik. Or was he still dreaming?

"Come on, Reuven, let's go!" Archik whispered.

Reuven scrambled to his feet. "I thought you had forgotten. You were fast asleep."

"Who, me? How could I sleep? I was just waiting until I was sure *they* were sleeping," Archik replied, jerking his head toward the snoring soldiers. "Did you expect me to make an announcement?"

"But you didn't move and...."

Archik's no-nonsense expression short-circuited Reuven's sentence.

"Leave the blanket, Reuven, we're traveling light."

"But it's freezing!" he protested, reluctantly dropping the flimsy fabric he had wrapped about him.

"The less we take, the better."

For the first fifty yards the two boys crawled on their stomachs, their heads low to the ground, their movements muffled by mud. Only when they were well away from the campsite did they stand up and run.

The boys stumbled into a black forest thick with branches of huge sycamores and elms. Low-lying brambles clawed at their arms and legs, thorns and nettles shredded their clothing.

A breathless Reuven pleaded with Archik to stop. "I

can't go on," he gasped, struggling manfully to keep up with his friend.

"We can't stop now," answered Archik, also breathless. "They'll soon be after us."

In a clearing just ahead of them, strands of light revealed the coming of dawn.

"Come on, Reuven," Archik begged. "I can already hear the river!"

As they pushed through a thicket, Reuven stopped in his tracks. "Do you hear what I hear?"

The sound of barking dogs rang through the forest.

"That's all we need," Archik moaned.

The barking grew louder. Archik grabbed Reuven's arm and pulled him forward.

"We'll never make it!" Reuven cried, surrender in his voice.

"Come on! They don't have us yet. The river's got to be around here somewhere. The map showed a small tributary of the Dvina at the edge of the forest."

"You and your maps," Reuven muttered.

A ribbon of light glittered through the thicket.

"Look, it's over there!" Archik exclaimed. "We've made it, we've made it!" he said, forcing his way through the brush.

A misty dawn revealed a dark, forbidding river flowing below them. Archik motioned for Reuven to plunge in. The dogs' barking grew louder. Reuven hesitated, then dove into the biting cold water, closely followed by Archik. The two boys struggled against the current.

"Can you swim?" Archik sputtered.

"Now you ask?" Reuven called back.

"Stay near," Archik shouted, but his words were cut short as his mouth filled with water.

"Grab on!" Reuven cried, as he saw a large log drift their way.

Archik thrashed about, but the log slipped from his grasp. The undercurrent gave no quarter and Archik felt himself going under.

With his last surge of energy, straining every muscle and nerve, Reuven reached his friend and pushed him onto the log. Spent from the exertion, he clung to the wood, bobbing in the freezing water until his stamina returned and he heaved himself astride.

The two clung to the massive, life-saving log for hours as the silver-black river snaked and curved, carrying them from the cold dawn to the warming midday sun.

Corporal Kolchak's florid face could not hide his fear as he stood at attention before Lieutenant Danikan. Perspiration poured down his brow, and he blinked in a fruitless effort to keep the drops out of his eyes. As Lieutenant Danikan glared at him from behind his desk, Corporal Kolchak tried desperately to draw upon his native shrewdness to dredge up an excuse for allowing two cantonists to escape, but this time his peasant brain refused to cooperate.

Earlier in the day, he felt he had credibly explained

the gaffe to the less formidable Sergeant Karenin, pointing out that the hostile terrain had forced them to make camp just short of the next town. "The weather was so bad that my men refused to go a step further. Even the horses balked," he had declared. "Believe me, Sergeant, it was impossible for two half-starved Yids to escape. You know the forests here." He then recounted to Sergeant Karenin every move he'd made from the very moment he'd discovered the two conscripts were gone. "I called in the local police and their dogs. And I led the search party myself. But it was no use," he said, shaking his head. "The Yids disappeared into thin air, like ghosts."

Kolchak now stood forlornly before the dreaded Lieutenant Danikan, whose reputation for cruelty was legendary. The lieutenant stalked toward him and the corporal's shoulders sagged.

"You incompetent halfwit! How could two wet-nosed conscripts escape the might of the Czarist army?" Danikan bellowed, jabbing his forefinger into Corporal Kolchak's chest. "I hold you personally responsible for their capture. Do you understand? Personally responsible! Cantonists are the Czar's property. Through your incompetence, you have lost the Czar's property. Worse, you have allowed two little Yids to outwit the Russian army!"

Lieutenant Danikan stomped across the room in a fury. Suddenly, spewing forth a string of curses and threats, he whirled about and stood with his legs astride and his hands on his hips.

"For the sake of the honor of the corps and the

reputation of the Russian army, I will be charitable," he said through clenched teeth, his face livid. "I am giving you a second chance, Kolchak. Find those Jews or else. And you are to bring them to me, do you understand?" He paused for a moment to catch his breath, then barked, "And I am posting a reward of fifty rubles a head for their capture, a reward that will come out of your salary!"

Corporal Kolchak swallowed hard. One hundred rubles, he thought. This was his reward for a lifetime of service? But all he dared say was, "I swear to you by all that is holy, I will find those boys, sir."

"Oh, you will indeed. For if you do not," said the lieutenant, now standing face to face with Corporal Kolchak, "a court-martial will decide your future. And it will be a future filled with grief, I assure you, if it is any future at all."

Returning to his desk, Lieutenant Danikan sifted through a sheaf of papers and held one to the light. "Out of allegiance to our corps," he snarled, "and to insure that you have no excuse for failure, I am assigning four men to join you in your search. Four men to find two Jews," he spat out. "Just remember, Corporal, I expect Reuven Fenster and Aharon Leib Gottlieb to be found."

Chapter 2

THE TWO BOYS drifted downriver for most of the day, too exhausted to even think about where they were headed—and what they would eat until they got there. They were free, and every moment took them farther from their captors. For now, that was enough.

While Reuven dozed, Archik rested his head on the log, watching the spring sun slowly fade into the horizon. He gazed dreamily into the orange-red rays, his mind for once free of all thoughts and plans. Suddenly, the sound of shouts shattered his reverie. In the distance he saw the splashing of a swimmer in trouble. Archik tensed, then dove into the water, his strong strokes taking him toward what were now distinct calls for help.

A young boy was flailing helplessly in the water. Archik made a grab for him, but the terrified child locked his arms about his neck, pulling them both down. Archik grappled to free himself from the boy's tight grasp. At last he managed to grab his hair and pull him to the log, where Reuven dragged the child up to safety. Drained from the effort, the boys managed to foot-paddle the log to shore, where they were met by a relieved peasant, his arms extended to grasp the whimpering child to his breast.

"Come with me," the peasant sputtered, his tears falling into his lush, red beard. Reuven and Archik glanced at each other, hastily appraising the situation. They had no choice but to follow.

The lads stumbled after the peasant up a steep hill. At the top, they stopped in their tracks, stunned. A handsome, two-story *dacha*, looking every inch the summer home of a noble, rose before them. The peasant waved them down a gravel path between tall junipers, past herb gardens, and finally into a huge kitchen.

"Nadia," he barked, "get these boys cleaned up and into dry clothes." Without another word he carried the child away.

The peasant woman bustled to do the man's bidding, and soon the boys sank deep into steaming tubs of water, scrubbing away months of grime with sweet-smelling soap. Soaking in the massive tubs, their aching muscles soothed by the warm water, they paid no heed to the commotion outside. They barely heard the shouts and the slamming door.

Pulling on the rough, clean peasant clothing the woman had left them, they gazed into the mirror. Reuven saw a handsome, sun-bronzed young man with wavy, dark brown hair and dark brown eyes. Archik stood beside him, the grime removed to reveal a handsome young lad with cornsilk ringlets crowning a sensitive, oddly aristocratic face.

There was a timid knock at the door, and the peasant woman entered and hustled them back into the kitchen. Sweet cream, fresh bread smeared with butter, and thick milk awaited them. Reuven and Archik gazed hungrily at the food. It had been so long since they had seen anything but stale bread and watery soup. Hunger had dogged them over so many miles. The boys now ate their first real meal in months. They washed, recited *motzi* softly, and devoured the food before them, mumbling *birkas hamazon* with feeling afterward.

"Stefan, I think they look presentable enough," Nadia cackled, rubbing her reddened hands on her ample white apron.

Led into a large sitting room, the boys stood gaping at the princely furnishings. There were several comfortable, chintz-covered settees and chairs. Along the walls were rosewood cabinets holding curios of jade and porcelain, and paintings of regal-looking men and elegant women—undoubtedly their host's ancestors—flanked by Venetian mirrors. A delicate spinet stood in one corner, gleaming in the sunlight that filtered through the creamy silk curtains dressing the huge windows. French doors opened onto carefully trimmed lawns surrounded by hedges pruned into fanciful designs. Tables set on the lawn were shaded by brightly colored umbrellas, and a pink and white gazebo stood in the distance. They drank in the opulence in silent awe as they waited in front of a carved walnut desk. Time seemed to unfold at a snail's pace.

When the door at the far end of the room finally opened, the boys jumped to military attention. A youngish, clean-shaven man with a wide, sensitive mouth entered. He was of medium height, and his thick mane of black hair was brushed straight back. His eyes were almost hidden by round glasses that gave him the appearance of a kindly owl. He introduced himself as Count Andre Kropotkin.

The boys stared, not knowing what to say.

"Children can cause their parents no end of heartache," the count said with a pleasant grin. "I brought my son, Nikolai, with me while inspecting my country home and leaving summer instructions for my staff. Not one minute out of my sight, and my naughty nine-year-old took it upon himself to test the water early in the season."

Archik glanced sideways at Reuven, who licked his lips nervously.

The count approached Archik. "My servant tells me that you are the lad who risked his life to save my son?"

Archik swallowed hard. "I only did what was right in the eyes of God, sir," he replied hoarsely.

"And what is your name, child?"

"Aharon Leib Gottlieb, sir."

"And your name?" Count Kropotkin asked, turning to a trembling Reuven.

"Reuven Fenster, sir."

"Stefan also said that from your uniforms he knows

you are the runaway cantonists being hunted by the army and police."

The boys could not conceal their fear.

The count smiled reassuringly. "Now, now, no need to worry. I have no sympathy for the heartless Cantonist Laws."

Startled but still uncertain, the boys breathed somewhat easier.

"Come, lads, sit down. We have much to talk about," the count said, indicating one of the delicate floral settees.

The boys hesitated and then sat down timidly.

"Have you had enough to eat?"

They nodded.

The count rose and languidly poured himself a glass of Madeira wine. He sipped slowly, appraising his guests.

"Now tell me, what are your plans? Where were you heading?"

Archik overcame the tightness in his throat and spoke: "We have placed ourselves in the hands of God, sir."

"You mean you ran off without any plan?"

"Not exactly, sir. I hope to somehow sail westward down the Dvina."

The count nodded, his expression solemn. "You both know that your chances of escaping dressed in conscript uniforms are very slim."

"I had hoped we could somehow rid ourselves of the uniforms."

“And how did you envision yourselves doing that?”

“As I said, sir, we have placed ourselves in the hands of God,” Archik replied.

The count chuckled good-naturedly. “I am very much indebted to you. You see, Aharon Leib, the boy you saved is my eldest, the future count. I hear that you rescued him without any thought for your own safety. And now, meeting you, I feel that you did your good deed out of the purest motives.”

His fingers steepled thoughtfully under his chin, the count spoke in a low, musing voice. “I will help you as best as I can.” He looked momentarily at the boys. “I had given serious thought to having you both join my staff here, but I abandoned that idea when a group of soldiers came by looking for you.”

Reuven glanced anxiously at Archik.

“You were quite fortunate to be out of their way, scrubbing yourselves clean. A corporal by the name of Kolchak offered a reward of one hundred rubles for the two of you.”

They gasped, exchanging stricken looks.

The count observed them quietly for a moment. “Fortunately, my servants are loyal to me. As for Nadia, she is not easily intimidated, and she knew exactly what to tell them. For the moment, they will be off your trail. But I am afraid that even under my roof your safety is not assured. Servants gossip, you understand, and you never know who’s listening.”

The count stared at the boys, as if sizing them up.

"I see you are still uncertain of me. Let me put your fears to rest. Although I am a Russian nobleman, I have spent most of my adult years traveling through Europe. I have been living in France for several years now, but I returned home recently at the request of my family. Someone had to look after our estates," he said with a shrug. "I have a great fondness for France," he continued, suddenly wistful. "Not only for French culture, but for the spirit of the revolution. Perhaps you lads have heard of the French Revolution of 1789?"

The count proceeded to lecture them, not waiting for a reply.

"It was a watershed in history. For a brief moment the common man held his destiny in his own hands. The revolution may have died with Bonaparte, but its ideals still stir the hearts and minds of the French people. Liberty, equality, fraternity—these ideals cannot be easily forgotten. Unfortunately, they have not made their way to Mother Russia." The count paused. Having all but forgotten about the boys, he seemed to be talking to himself. "I feel certain that if only our Czar had progressive advisors who would let some fresh air into his court, he, too, would fall in step with the nineteenth century. But, alas, they keep him in the dark," he said with a deep sigh, absolving the monarch of his sins.

"I admit that not many noblemen share my views. Unfortunately, the majority of Russian aristocracy will not move one inch in the direction of enfranchisement. Oh, how we hold fast to our rule! By the time we awaken, it will be too late and we shall be forced to pay a heavy price. History, my lads, is not on the side of princes," he concluded, shaking his head.

The silence of the moment was broken only by the sound of the count pouring wine into his crystal goblet and the distant crowing of a rooster. The count shrugged, then chuckled. His face seemed to lighten up.

"For the moment I imagine that these momentous historical events are of little concern to you. So let us turn to our first order of business—keeping you out of the clutches of the police and army." He pursed his lips in thought. "To insure your safety, you'll have to pretend to be peasant boys. Aharon Leib, I think my son's first name would suit you very well. If you are ever questioned, say that you are Nikolai Vasilovich Dudorov. Can you remember that?"

Archik swallowed hard. "Yes. My name is Nikolai Vasilovich Dudorov."

"From Volchov."

"Volchov?"

"Yes," the count winked mischievously. "Far north and remote. It is doubtful that you will ever meet anyone from there.

"As for Reuven, let me see," he said, stroking his chin. "You are now...Yuri Pavlovich Gorki."

Reuven's jaw tightened.

"Reuven, can you repeat that name? It must come naturally to your lips."

Reuven stammered, "Yuri Pavlovich Gorki."

"Fine, that will do," the count announced, obviously satisfied.

"How do we make our way west?" Archik asked, his old, unruffled self surfacing.

"Ah, yes," the count grinned. "I will instruct Stefan to build a sturdy raft tonight. It just would not do for peasant boys to be seen traveling in style, would it now?"

Archik nodded in agreement. "But what if we are stopped and questioned. What are we to say? What are we doing so far from Volchov?"

Count Kropotkin smiled, amused. "When you ran off without a plan, it appears that no such questions troubled you."

Archik looked steadily at the count. "When we fled, sir, we put ourselves in the hands of the Almighty. Now He has placed us in your hands, sir."

The count guffawed and rubbed his neck. "Indeed. Well, in that case a great responsibility has been thrust upon me. Let's just say, you are looking for work. Russia is always in the throes of economic upheaval and the situation in the north is particularly grave. It's not unusual for peasant workers to travel in search of bread."

Both boys smiled for the first time. The count rose and extended his manicured hand to the lads. "Go with God."

They spent the night as guests of Count Kropotkin. Awakened by Stefan at dawn, they davened *shacharis*, then followed him dutifully back to the river. There, to their amazement, they found a fine raft waiting for them, complete with a small tarpaulin tent in the middle to protect them from the elements. Inside the tent were knapsacks and bundles of utensils, food, and clothing.

Before bidding them farewell, Stefan handed Archik a compass. He then placed leather pouches about their necks.

"The good count has given you enough money to keep you in provisions for your journey. Be careful of highwaymen and scoundrels, my lads," he said as he pushed them off. "And may God protect you and give you fair sailing."

They waved back and smiled, paying little attention to the thick blanket of black clouds gathering above.

Chapter 3

REUVEN AND ARCHIK huddled together under the raft's tent. Streaks of lightning flashed across the sky, and torrential rain and gale-force winds tossed their small craft.

"Do you think we should try for the shore?" Reuven asked between chattering teeth as the taste of bile rose in his throat.

"We're still too close to the search party for comfort. I don't think they've given up on us yet, not with a price on our heads and Corporal Kolchak on our trail. Let's try to stay on the river as long as we can."

"But how safe are we out here?"

"Safer."

The boys recited the *Shema* more than once as the river's raging waters threatened to tear their raft apart. When at last the rain slackened to a drizzle and the raft fell into a pleasant drift, the wet but grateful lads thanked God for having survived the tempest. When the sun began peeking out from behind the rapidly moving clouds, Reuven hoped they would head for land, but Archik refused.

"We're still too near our guards. For all we know, the entire army and police force may be hunting for us by now."

Reuven considered his younger friend's words. He knew that danger lurked on shore. On the other hand, the river hardly guaranteed their safety. On the contrary, it teemed with barges and ferries loaded with timber, coal, iron, and westbound passengers. For the moment, though, he agreed that the river was probably safer than the shore that beckoned so invitingly.

In his usual imperious manner, Archik soon set up what he called a "survival plan."

"We must take stock and ration our food supplies," he instructed Reuven, as if counseling a child. "Our provisions won't last indefinitely and we have no way of knowing when we will find more."

Reuven swallowed the retort that rose to his lips. For the moment, at least, he would humor his pompous junior companion.

"Later on we'll take turns cleaning the raft. And Reuven," he declared sternly, "we must bathe in the river daily, and launder our clothes. We may look like *goyim* but we can't allow ourselves to turn into peasants."

Reuven eyed Archik closely. The road ahead was long and difficult enough and he was determined not to fall prey to petty disagreements.

The weather turned unseasonably warm and the river became tranquil. Days drifted into one another with the gentle bobbing of the raft.

A sixth sense kept Reuven from intruding upon the privacy of his taciturn companion. Instead, he yawned lazily. Resting his head on his knapsack, he gazed up at the sky. The river sparkled aquamarine and the air was spiced with the aroma of spring flowers. He let his hand dangle in the cool water, and watched a line of cotton barges churn by as a ferry paddled passengers from one river port to another. "I wonder what my mother would say if she could see her son now, dressed like a *goy*, sailing downriver," Reuven said, half to himself. Then he looked at Archik and laughed. "My father won't know what to make of you, Archik, but my mother will only want to fatten you up."

"You are a dreamer, Reuven," Archik interrupted gruffly.

"What do you mean?"

"Just what I said. You haven't once asked why I keep checking the compass. Or in what direction the raft is drifting. Doesn't it matter to you?"

"Of course it matters," he answered, startled at Archik's harsh tone.

"Do you think I plan for us to head right back into the mouth of the Russian bear? You talk about a reunion with your parents, but where is your *shtetl*? More than five hundred miles east, through totally hostile territory!"

The color drained from Reuven's face. "Maybe it was

wishful thinking, Archik, but it was my dream. You know how I want to see my parents, yet in all these weeks, you've never once said, 'Reuven, we can't go in that direction.' Was that fair to me?"

Archik turned a deep crimson and mumbled something under his breath.

"What is it, Archik?" Reuven demanded sharply.

For once, Archik's words came slowly and with difficulty. "I wanted you to come with me. I guess that's why I let you think you were going home. Besides, I really thought that in your heart you knew the truth, and in time you'd stop talking about your family."

"Maybe you are right," Reuven shrugged. "Maybe I was deluding myself. I just hoped that freedom would somehow enable me to return home. I still pray for such a miracle. In the end it is in Hashem's hands. But in the meantime, do me one favor: stop this childish secretiveness. Once and for all, I want to know—where we are we going?"

The corners of Archik's mouth turned down. Scowling, he blurted out, "Lithuania."

"Lithuania? Then we *are* heading into the mouth of the bear. You know the Cantonist Laws extend into Lithuania."

Archik reddened. "You don't have to lecture me," he replied angrily. "And you don't have to come all the way with me, either. Look, you have every right to be annoyed, but I was going to tell you my plan long before we reached our destination. I figured that once we made it to the border you could head to the safety of Latvia."

"I don't understand," Reuven said, shaking his head. "You have parents in the Ukraine. If you are going to place yourself in danger, why not head for home?"

"I wish I could explain it to you now, but all I can say is that I must reach my aunt and uncle in Kovno in Lithuania. And it has nothing to do with escaping the Czar."

"If it isn't a hiding place you're looking for, then what is it?"

"I'm sorry, Reuven, but I can't say any more. Just believe me: I have no choice but to go there."

Reuven scratched his head, bewildered.

Archik turned over onto his stomach, resting his head on his arms. "If you want to come along with me," he said with a sidelong glance at his companion, "I...that is, I wouldn't mind. Besides, I really don't think the army will follow us to Lithuania. They've probably given up on us already. After all, what are two insignificant Jewish conscripts to them anyway?"

"I hope you're right," Reuven replied, not entirely convinced.

Reuven clutched his knees under his chin, eyeing Archik. Once again, he tried to understand his friend. Throughout their difficult month together Archik had remained a closed book. How did a boy so young develop such a well-honed sense of survival? He was so cheerful, so cocky, so self-confident, yet he could be sulky and underhanded as well. And always, there was an air of reserve, almost of secrecy, surrounding him. He had to admit that the chutzpah that made Archik so hard to live with was sometimes admirable. After all, without it they never would have escaped.

Reuven smiled wanly. "Of course, I'll go with you to Lithuania. We're partners, aren't we?"

Archik tried to hide the relief on his face.

"In that case, Reuven, do you want to look at the route we're taking?"

"Of course."

Archik pulled out the dog-eared map and unfolded it. "Look," he said, tracing his finger along a curving line. "If we're lucky we'll drift right along the Dvina, and that should take us to the border."

"Phew! That's some trip for a raft."

"We'll make it," Archik said with a wave of his hand. "We've got to make it."

"Will the river take us to Kovno?"

"No," Archik grinned, "but close enough. We'll go overland when we get to Zarasai," he said, his finger marking the border of Lithuania. "You'll enjoy the walk after sitting around for so long." The boy proudly cocked his head. "It's a good plan, Reuven. I'll get us there, don't you worry."

Reuven looked at his friend. "With Hashem's help," he gently intoned.

That evening, Reuven turned to the piece of bark they used to record the days, a simple method he had devised to mark when Shabbos was. "Tomorrow is Friday," he observed.

"Well," Archik said, "I guess tomorrow morning

we'll pull into shore."

The next morning they awoke to a pale sun, which was soon hidden behind a barricade of clouds. The current had turned swift, and it took all their skill to paddle to shore. When they were almost aground, they leaped overboard and pulled the water-logged raft up onto the riverbank. After taking off just enough food and supplies for Shabbos, they dragged the raft under the hanging branches of a large willow tree. "I think the raft can still be seen," Reuven remarked nervously.

"You're right, for a change," Archik agreed with a playful grin.

They gathered branches and handfuls of leaves, piling them high to cover the raft. When it was well hidden, they began walking through the woods in search of shelter. The wind was rising and the air was heavy with the smell of rain.

Their feet sank into the muddy ground as they trudged through the dark forest. In the cultivated fields of some nameless nobleman, they saw several peasants preparing the loamy soil for seeding. One peasant wearing a well-patched shirt waved at them. They waved back. He looked up at the sky, put some spittle on his fingertips, and held them up to the air. Then he shook his head and called out, "Be careful, lads, there's a storm brewing." They shouted back their thanks over the fierce wind.

"We'd better find shelter before the storm hits," Archik said.

They climbed over a rocky hill, which led to a stand of huge conifers. "Over here!" Reuven cried.

Archik found Reuven standing before the yawning mouth of a cave. They peered into the dark, dank, uninviting interior. A clap of thunder and pelting rain helped them regain their courage, and they cautiously entered the darkness.

"It's pitch black in here," Reuven whispered.

"Wait, I'll light the lanterns."

Using dry flint Archik lit the oil lamps they had taken from the raft. A dozen flying objects swooshed past them in a mad escape from the light. Archik shrieked.

"It's only bats," Reuven said between clenched teeth.

"There may be more dangerous animals inside," Archik warned, recoiling at the thought. "Like bears."

"We'll find out soon enough," Reuven said, trying to sound brave.

"What will we do then?"

"Then," Reuven managed a grin, "we'll recite the *Shema*."

Rushing ahead into the cave, Archik soon forgot his fears as he stared in wonder at this new, hidden world with its fantastic array of stalactites and stalagmites. He turned to share his excitement with Reuven—but he was nowhere in sight.

Panic-stricken, Archik called out Reuven's name, only to hear it reverberating throughout the maze of cavernous rooms. He turned to retrace his steps, but suddenly he was slipping down, down. He grabbed at air, and caught hold of a ledge. His legs dangled precariously in space. Having dropped his precious lantern, he had plunged into total darkness.

Once again Archik called his friend's name, but his voice was weak and thin. His body ached and his hands grew raw from the jutting limestone. With all his strength he pulled himself up over the ledge. His hand grasped something that felt solid. He took a deep breath, muttered a prayer, and hoisted his body onto solid ground, releasing one scraped hand to grope for leverage. After a moment's rest, he drew himself to his feet.

Darkness engulfed him. Archik knew he had two choices: to remain glued to where he stood, or to continue his search for his friend. He shuddered and took a cautious step, then a second and a third, probing his way. His heart beat rapidly. He realized that each step could be his last. For all he knew he could be walking in circles, or standing at the edge of a precipice. Archik strained against the darkness, hoping to clutch a glimmer of light. Drawing upon every last ounce of stamina, Archik began calling his friend's name. The minutes seemed like hours. There was no reply. In despair Archik sank to the ground, certain that he would never find his friend or his way out of the cave.

Did he hear something, or was it only his heartbeat? Very slowly he pulled himself to his feet. No, he was certain he had heard a sound. Was it his name? He put his ear close to the cavern wall. Again he heard it, and this time there was no doubt.

"Archik! Archik!"

He exhaled a long-held breath.

"Archik, do you hear me?"

"I'm here!" he shouted in return.

"Don't move, just keep calling my name."

Archik's sigh of relief resounded like a thousand tambourines. In a moment, Reuven was standing by his side.

They fell into each other's arms, both too frightened and exhausted to do anything but sink to the damp ground.

"I thought this was the end of me," Archik admitted. "And it was so dark!"

The experience now became an anecdote and they both laughed at the adventure, repeating every detail with relish.

Archik threw his arm about Reuven's shoulders. "From now on we lock arms. No moving about alone. Just hold tight and follow me," he said with regained bravado. "You've got to see those huge pillars. They're incredible!"

"Not now, Archik. We've had enough excitement for one day."

"But Reuven, you just have to see what I saw inside those caverns. It was unbelievable!"

Reuven stood his ground. "No more exploring for today. Besides, we have to prepare for Shabbos."

Reluctantly Archik placed their remaining lantern on the ground and they both searched for the driest spot on which to spend Shabbos. The boys had packed dry tinder and Archik built a fire large enough to cook food and provide some warmth and additional light. The boys had long ago committed their *tefillos* to memory, and as evening fell they once again thanked Hashem for sparing their lives.

No sooner had they finished davening when Reuven drew back, grabbing Archik's arm. There could be no doubt: peering out of a dark corner were two gleaming eyes.

"*Ribono shel olam*," Reuven gasped, "it's a wild animal!"

"Shh," Archik whispered. "You stay here. I'll try to get a closer look."

"Don't be foolish. Let's get out of here."

But Archik was already heading toward the glittering eyes, reassuring Reuven that the fire would keep the beast away. Suddenly he heard a whimper of fear.

"Please, please don't hurt me," a high-pitched voice quavered.

A lad appeared out of the darkness. He seemed no older than Archik, though it was hard to tell with his face covered in grime and his clothing wet and muddy. But not even the mud could disguise a uniform of a conscript.

Reuven chuckled. "A cantonist!"

"Please, I beg you, have mercy! Don't turn me in! Here, here," the boy said, stuffing his hands into his jacket pocket. "I have a few kopeks," he pleaded. "Take them. Just don't send me back."

Reuven glanced at the lad, his throat tight. He touched the boy's shoulder lightly.

"You have nothing to fear. We are also runaway conscripts. Now why don't you come closer and warm yourself by the fire."

The terrified lad edged back, his gaze darting warily from one boy to the other.

"Don't let our clothing fool you. Didn't you hear us daven?"

The child seemed bewildered. "I heard you, but I couldn't make out what you were saying. How do I know that you are really Jews?"

The two laughed. "*Mir zeinen Yidden.* Now do you believe us?"

Sinking to the ground, the conscript covered his face with his grimy hands and wept.

When he calmed himself, they suggested that he use the gathered rainwater to wash. Since there was no wine, they recited a heartfelt *kiddush* over their bread before beginning their simple Shabbos meal. Reuven served the starved boy the largest portion.

"I'm Yussel Poznansky from Chortkov," he began shyly.

"Aharon Leib Gottleib," Archik introduced himself, offering a hearty handshake.

"But you can call him Archik," Reuven interjected. "And I'm Reuven Fenster."

"I can't thank you enough for sharing your Shabbos meal with me."

Reuven smiled. "No need to thank us, Yussel. We are happy to have an *orayach* for Shabbos. Tell us, how did you ever get here?"

"Well," Yussel drawled, "I guess the best place to start is when I became a cantonist. Like many other boys in my village, I was conscripted right after my twelfth birthday. They came and dragged me out of my home. I was so frightened and confused that to this day I don't remember where they took me," he said, wiping away a tear.

"By now you know the routine. They tried to starve and beat us into becoming *goyim*. Some caved in, others died, and I just held on as best as I could. When they saw I wouldn't budge, they sent me off to slave for some peasant. That was over two years ago. And he was even worse than the soldiers. At least in the canton, there were other Jewish boys and we encouraged each other. With the peasant I was alone and I lived like an animal, locked in a barn at night.

"I knew that if he couldn't get me baptised he would kill me. What choice did I have but to try to escape? I worked on that lock every night, and one night it clicked open and I ran away. The peasant's land was near a river, and that gave me an idea. I remember my father telling me that a man was required to teach his son Torah, a trade, and how to swim. At that time I had no idea why swimming was so important, but now..." he said with a grin, "well, I appreciate his lessons. When I saw the river I dived in and swam until my arms and legs wouldn't move anymore. I made it to shore and wandered through the countryside until I found this cave."

Yussel smiled, then suddenly put his hands over his

mouth to suppress a gasp. "Wait a minute. When I was passing through a small village, I saw... on a poster...."

"Poster? What poster?" Reuven asked.

"It said: `<S>REWARD FOR ESCAPED CANTONISTS.' I thought it might be about me, but it gave your names, and there was also a description. The army is offering fifty rubles for each of you."

"*Guttenyu*," Archik murmured.

Reuven shook his head ruefully. They had de-luded themselves into thinking they had escaped their pursuers, but they were being hunted like criminals.

He gazed at Yussel and forced a smile. After all, this was Shabbos and Yussel was their guest.

"Yussel, you are welcome to travel with us."

"Where are you heading?"

"West," Archik replied vaguely.

Yussel appeared to waver and then he shook his head. "No, but thanks anyway. I'm going south heading to Odessa."

"Odessa?"

"My grandfather went to Eretz Yisrael as an old man," Yussel said with a shy grin. "He now lives in Yerushalayim. At home I used to read his letters, each one filled with holiness and joy."

"You mean he never wrote to you about the poverty of the Jews and the cruelty of the Ottomans?" Archik exclaimed.

"Yes, of course he wrote about the difficulties of life under Turkish rule. But my grandfather said that it really didn't matter as long as he was learning Torah in Yerushalayim."

Yussel rubbed his hands over the embers, trying to grasp every drop of warmth. "To me all that matters now is that one day I will sit at my grandfather's side and study with him. If life is hard there, well, it certainly isn't *Gan Eden* here," he observed with a grimace. "I pray that Hashem will help me get to Odessa and from there, with His help, I will somehow get to Eretz Yisrael."

Reuven smiled faintly and patted Yussel's shoul-der. "That shouldn't be too difficult. Nowadays there is a ferry that sails from Odessa to Yafo."

"*Baruch Hashem*!" Yussel cried, his eyes gleaming with hope.

Yussel and Reuven spent most of Shabbos talking about themselves.

"I'm from the village of Kabaney, in Kiev Gubernya," Reuven sighed, nostalgia overcoming him. "My father was a *shneider*, a tailor, and to be a *shneider* in Kabaney meant to be hungry most of the time. After all, what work was there for him but a patch here and a patch there? He was a fine tailor but no one could afford a new suit or dress. There was never much money, but our home was filled with Torah. I can still see my mother preparing for Shabbos. The house sparkled and the table was set with a beautiful white linen tablecloth my mother had inherited from her mother, with her mother's initials embroidered in the middle. To me, it seemed as if our Shabbos meal was a fit for a king. There was always black bread, herring, and potatoes—a feast.

"I would watch my father work, and no matter how many hours he spent sewing, after supper he would study. Some people look down on tailors as being ignorant, but that wasn't true of my father. Though he spent his entire day working, he knew a lot. My mother always worried that my father would lose his eyesight, what with bending over his sewing all day and his *sefarim* all night. But he would wave her away, insisting that besides his family, learning was his only pleasure. My mother would shake her head, and even though I was only a child, I could see the pride in her eyes."

"My father was the village *shochet*," Yussel began, blinking his eyes as if bringing the memory into clearer focus. "It seems like such a long time ago," he murmured wistfully. "We also owned a small shop where my mother sold cloth and buttons and things like that. My brother and sisters and I helped my mother whenever we could, though my father insisted that we go to *cheder* and spend most of our time studying. You know, even though we didn't have much money, my father engaged a *melamed* to review with us what we learned in *cheder*, and to teach us things our *cheder melamed* did not have time for."

Archik listened to the two boys, but as usual kept his thoughts to himself.

After *havdalah*, they packed their belongings back into a sack.

"Let's not take any chances. We mustn't leave a trace of our presence," Archik proclaimed with typical authority. He agreed to leave only when he was absolutely satisfied that there was no evidence of their stay in the cave.

They walked out into the cool night air. The sky had cleared and the stars shone with extraordinary brilliance. Suddenly Archik grabbed Yussel by the shoulders and inspected him as if seeing him for the very first time. "Yussel, you can't travel in that conscript's uniform!"

"Do I have a choice?"

Archik put down his knapsack and pulled out some of the peasant clothing Count Kropotkin had given them.

Yussel hesitated. "But those are your clothes. You'll need whatever you have for your journey."

"We have more than enough of everything."

"You can believe him," Reuven urged. "But there is something you can do for us in repayment."

Yussel smiled wanly. "I can't imagine how I can possibly repay both of you for your generosity and kindness. All I have are those few kopeks."

"Since we have absolute faith that you will soon stand before the *Kosel* in Yerushalayim, we ask you to remember us and place a *kvittel*, a petition, in the *Kosel* for us."

Yussel's eyes clouded with tears and he swallowed hard. "Yes, I would be happy to perform that mitzvah."

"And we promise that we will pray with all of our hearts for your safe journey and your reunion with your grandfather in Eretz Yisrael. Now there is another thing to be done."

Reuven pulled a handful of rubles out of the leather pouch hanging around his neck and pressed the money into Yussel's hand. "I wish we could give you all our money, Yussel, but we have no way of knowing what the future has in store for us. I hope this will help you get to Yerushalayim."

"But where, how..." the choked words trailed off.

"Don't worry, Yussel, the money was honestly earned, believe me."

"I don't understand."

"Let's just say that Hashem works in strange ways."

Archik clasped Yussel's shoulder. "We're not finished with you yet, my friend. Reuven, I ask you, how is Yussel going to make it to Odessa?"

Reuven clapped the palm of his hand to his forehead. "You mean we're going to build a raft for him as well?"

"Either that or he'll have to walk to Eretz Yisrael!"

The three lads raced down to the river. They worked at a feverish pace picking up driftwood and branches that yesterday's storm had washed ashore. By dawn, they had put together a modest raft. Yussel studied it dubiously, and it took all of Reuven and Archik's powers of persuasion to get him to climb aboard.

Before sailing off, they davened *shacharis* together. Then the boys bid Yussel farewell, waving until their arms ached. Only then did they set out on their own journey, certain that their meeting with Yussel was a good omen.

Chapter 4

CLAD IN THEIR peasant clothing, the two lads wearily climbed a steep embankment, tugging their waterlogged raft behind them. A small clearing stretched before them.

"Can we make camp here? I hate the woods when it's dark," Reuven groaned.

"I guess so," Archik agreed warily.

For most of that week the weather had been blustery and the river choppy. Even though their sailing skills had improved, the boys longed for the feel of solid ground beneath their feet. Because of the rough current, they headed for shore on Thursday instead of Friday, hoping to find a Jewish community. At the very least, they would be able to restock their provisions.

As always, their first job was to conceal the raft. They placed it within an overgrown thicket, and then covered it with branches and leaves to complete the camouflage. Finally, well pleased with their efforts, they returned to the clearing and began to build a fire.

Suddenly, a raspy voice broke the silence of the countryside. "What are you doing here?" it snarled.

The boys whirled about. At the edge of the woods stood a knot of rough-looking men. They drew back in terror. Was one of the men Corporal Kolchak? "Only bandits," Archik whispered after a moment. Reuven smiled at the sound of relief in his voice, then his face grew sombre. These might not be the Czar's men, but they were clearly very dangerous.

A beefy, thick-featured man, his stomach hanging over pants tucked deep into muddy boots, held them in his bloodshot gaze. A rusty antique rifle was slung over his shoulder.

"What's your business here?" he barked.

Assuming a nonchalance he did not feel, Archik strode over. "We come from the north, from Volchov, looking for work," he said in what he hoped was an innocent, peasant-boy manner.

The leader appraised him coldly. "You sure you ain't some kind of nobleman's brat or somethin'?" he spat, eyeing Archik with poisonous interest. It suddenly dawned on Archik that being taken for an aristocrat was about as dangerous as being taken for a Jew. A chill crept up his back as he read the word "ransom" on the men's thieving faces. Desperate to keep up his pose, Archik threw his head back in laughter. "Some nobleman," he sputtered, pointing to their simple clothing.

The men moved off to the side, muttering among themselves, their faces a meshing of collective evil.

"So what do they call you?"

Archik caught Reuven's eye and indicated that he was to join him.

"Nikolai, Nikolai Vasilovich, and this is my friend Yuri Pavlovich."

Once again the men put their heads together, murmuring darkly. This time the leader motioned for the boys to follow. Shivering, and eyeing each other uneasily, they had no choice but to obey. The gang's campsite was well hidden in the heart of a grove of tall evergreens. The air was pungent with the stale smell of tobacco and vodka. Following the men's lead, the boys squatted around the leader, who answered to the name of Samoilov. He offered the boys a bowl of beet, potato, and cabbage stew that was the bandits' dinner. To avoid suspicion, Reuven and Archik accepted, barely concealing their sighs of relief that there was no meat in the stew.

After some debate, Samoilov turned to the boys. "So you two are looking for work?"

"Yes, sir," Archik replied.

"How'd you like to join up with us? We can always use two good men," he chuckled.

The invitation, they fearfully realized, was an order.

Fortunately, their youth excluded the boys from the gang's nightly drunken revelry. At least for the moment, they were left alone. Sleep had hardly overtaken the lads when they were unceremon-iously shaken back to wakefulness. A group of the bandits stood over them.

"Now it's time to learn how to earn your keep," Samoilov muttered, "and maybe even fill your empty pockets with silver and gold. About five miles south of here is the village of Zabori. It may look poor, but don't let that fool you. The Jews of Zabori are so stingy they live in shacks, like they ain't got a kopek between them. But we know better," he cackled, scratching his tangled beard and rubbing his hands together. "Believe me, they got gold and silver stashed away under the floorboards and in the cellars, and we aim to relieve them of their burdens," he laughed.

"Listen carefully and you'll never have to work for a living. The plan is to attack tomorrow night, on the eve of their Sabbath." He coughed several times and spat on the ground. "Now you boys ain't got nothin' to worry about. Yids never put up a fight, especially on their Sabbath. We'll make off with all of their silver and gold just like that," he said with a snap of his fingers. He leaned close to Archik, his foul breath and words making the boy wince. "All you two have to do is follow us into the houses and help carry out the loot. If you want to smash a few heads, it's okay," he winked, "but don't waste too much time. Not that the police care what we do to Jews. Got it?" he sniggered.

The boys nodded, licking their dry lips and trying to act unconcerned.

"You two just might turn into good thieves yet, if you got the stomach for it. Believe me, boys, you ain't never got to worry about going hungry if you stick with me. Ain't that right, fellows?" The men, half-dazed from vodka, managed to grunt affirmatively.

When the gang members finally fell into a drunken slumber, Archik cautiously edged closer to Reuven, who was lying on the hard ground, staring at the fire. He tapped him on the shoulder and placed a finger to his lips, then motioned for Reuven to follow him into the woods. When they were a safe distance from the snoring cutthroats, the boys stopped.

"Listen, Reuven, we've got to find that village and warn the Jews. If not, there will be a massacre. And we must do it tonight, or we may not have another chance!"

Reuven nodded his assent, and without another word the boys raced through the dense woods, for once indifferent to the fearsome sounds of baying wolves and the brambles tearing at their legs. With their compass as their guide, they arrived at the sleeping village well before dawn. Panting and shivering from exhaustion, they collapsed against a tree. They had run five miles without stopping.

Mopping his face with his shirtsleeve, Reuven gazed at the unsuspecting village. Samoilov was right about one thing: it looked pathetically poor. "Gold? Silver?" Reuven cried. "*Ribono shel olam*, where do they get their ideas?"

The boys dashed into the village in search of the rabbi's home, certain it would be close to the synagogue. They strained their eyes in the darkness, rushing up and down the unmarked alleys and lanes until they arrived at a small, wooden building with a menorah chiseled over the lintel.

"The shul," Reuven whispered.

They walked on to an adjoining building. A light flickered through a small window. Inside, they could make out the shadowy figure of a man sitting at a table, hunched over a *sefer*.

Archik made a thumbs-up sign, then motioned to Reuven. "Follow me," he said hoarsely.

They tapped on the door, lightly at first and then with greater urgency. At last the light of a lantern shimmered through the window. A middle-aged, portly man with a silver-tinged black beard opened the door a crack. At the sight of the two disheveled boys in peasant clothing, he was ready to slam the door shut, but Archik cried out, "*Mir zeinen Yidden*! We're Jews!" He was about to add that they were runaway conscripts as well when something within made him hold his tongue.

The door swung open and the man motioned for them to enter, his eyes round in astonishment. He invited the exhausted boys to sit down, and offered them water.

"Are you the rabbi of this village?" Reuven asked breathlessly.

"Yes, I am Rabbi Avigdor Saretsky."

In a rush of words, the boys told of their escape from the bandits. "Rabbi, they are planning a pogrom tonight!" Reuven blurted out.

The rabbi fell into a chair, gripping his head in his hands. "What do they want from us?" he wailed.

"Rabbi, something must be done," Archik stated gravely.

The rabbi stared ahead, absorbed in his thoughts. At last he rose and absently poured himself and the boys steaming glasses of tea from a battered samovar. As the rabbi drank silently, the boys had a chance to examine their surroundings. The immaculate two-room cottage wore its poverty with proud dignity. The furniture in the room that served as a kitchen, dining room, and study was spare and utilitarian: a few rickety chairs, a large oval table, a small desk, and a threadbare upholstered chair. The cupboard held simple crockery, a brass oil menorah, pewter candlesticks, and a wooden *besamim* box. Even the rabbi's library with its tattered *sefarim* bespoke grinding poverty.

The boys sipped the sweet tea and waited.

"My dear boys, may the *Ribono shel olam* bless you for what you have done," the rabbi began softly. "You have not forgotten your people. Your courage will be well rewarded in the World to Come. Now," he said, clasping his hands together, "I must consider the problem and weigh the alternatives."

"Is there nothing to be done?"

The rabbi offered a wan smile. "Of course there is something to be done. Hashem has given us our lives, and we are obligated to preserve them. Our wives and children will not be sacrificed, you can be certain." He lifted himself from his chair and paced the room, his fingers combing his beard.

Suddenly, Archik jumped to his feet.

"Rabbi Avigdor, perhaps the women and children can hide in the forest?"

"You are a clever lad, Aharon Leib. But when the pogromists find we have no gold and silver, they will burn our homes to the ground. Fortunate-ly, we have a few strong young men in our village, and I think those bandits are in for an unpleasant surprise," he said, a tight smile surfacing. "Have faith—Hashem will not permit such a calamity to befall us. You boys remain in my home for the time being," he instructed with a wave of his hand, "and I will have a talk with some of our young men. They will not run from a fight, you can be sure."

"Can we join them?" Archik asked eagerly.

"I don't know. You are both so young," the rabbi said, his face drawn into a frown.

"Rabbi Avigdor, they are a gang of eight," Reuven protested. "The more men you have to face them, the better. They may have weapons, but we will have the element of surprise. It's our *mazel* that they know nothing of the laws of *pikuach nefesh*, that we are allowed to defend our lives on Shabbos."

Rabbi Saretsky swayed to and fro, his eyes closed, as he weighed the boys' request. "Very well then. Now we have little time to waste."

Archik glanced at Reuven. "We had better get back to the camp. If they find us gone, who knows what they'll do. They must be taken completely by surprise."

"I will not permit you to return to that lions' den!" the rabbi exclaimed.

"But what if they get suspicious?"

The rabbi considered Archik's words for a moment. "They will probably just think you got fright-ened and ran off. It will never occur to them that you are Jews. Not the way you boys are dressed," he assured them.

For the next few hours Rabbi Saretsky worked ceaselessly, alerting the townspeople to the imminent danger and discussing defense tactics with the men. He returned home in the early morning, satisfied that the villagers had been well prepared. Only then did he wake the two exhausted boys.

The lads joined the *minyan* in shul for *shacharis*. The prospect of danger ahead could not dampen their joy when they put on the tefillin they'd borrowed from the rabbi. How long since they had tightened those leather straps around their arms!

They returned to the rabbi's home, and Rabbi Saretsky introduced them to the rebbetzin, briefly describing their mission. As she turned her full attention to feeding the hungry boys, the rabbi left the house without a further word.

Hours before Shabbos, the elderly, the women, and the children were bundled off into the nearby forest. Several men stood guard around them, armed with whatever household utensils they had. The younger, able-bodied villagers remained in the town, some in their homes, others positioned at the outskirts of the village, carrying the tools of their trades as weapons: axes, hammers, rolling pins, carving knives, and yardsticks. Ten men, including Archik and Reuven, acted as sentinels on the high points, ready to signal the others. The air seemed exceptionally still, and Reuven and Archik shivered.

Shortly after midnight they heard the muffled sound

of men threading their way through dense growth. The signal was given and the villagers moved swiftly in pincer formation. No sooner had the bandits entered the village than they were surrounded. Stunned by the show of force, and realizing they were outnumbered and outmaneuvered, the gang beat a hasty retreat, but not before Samoilov spotted the two lads. As he galloped off, they heard him vow vengeance.

That Shabbos was a memorable one for all. The boys were feted as heroes, and Rabbi Saretsky and his rebbetzin arranged for them to visit every villager's home. Each cottage was brimming with happiness, and though the refreshments were often meager, the joy they shared was plentiful.

After *havdalah* the rebbetzin packed some provisions for the lads. Rabbi Saretsky then sat down with them to share a few quiet moments. He leaned forward in his threadbare chair, opened the drawer of his desk, and drew out a package, which he handed to Reuven.

"This is a small token of our appreciation and affection."

Reuven and Archik hesitated.

"Come now, open it," the rabbi urged.

Reuven's fingers worked nervously at the well-secured cord. When he finally managed to open the package, the two gasped. Inside were two new *siddurim* and a *Chumash*.

"I am sorry we could not provide tefillin as well," the rabbi said with an apologetic smile. "We are a poor village, and have none to spare."

The rabbi cleared his throat and spoke again. "My dear boys," he said, "I am well aware that you are runaway cantonists. Word of your escape has reached even our small village."

Reuven flushed. Archik produced a cold smile.

"Have no fear of me or anyone in this village. I understand why you didn't tell me, and I'm not offended by your caution. Now perhaps you want to write to your parents to assure them that you are alive and well. I will do my best to see that your letters reach them."

Reuven rubbed his forehead, taking a moment to consider the rabbi's words. "Rabbi Avigdor, thank you for your offer. I have thought long and hard about finding a way to contact my parents, and I know Archik has done the same. But," he took a deep breath, "such a letter might lead the army to its source." He hesitated a moment. "In the end it could cause greater grief than joy."

Rabbi Saretsky passed the back of his hand over his eyes to hide his emotions. "You are far wiser than your years. May it be Hashem's will that one day you again eat at your fathers' tables."

The next morning, the rabbi and a delegation of young men from the village accompanied them to the river, where their well-hidden raft awaited them.

"My dear children, may Hashem guard you and bless you on your journey," the rabbi said in a trembling voice. "I beg of you, be very cautious. In his madness, the Czar has increased his quota of children to be conscripted into the army. Every year, more boys are dragged from their homes. What will be the end, only Hashem knows. For safety's sake, keep your identity secret whenever possible. *Ba-ruch Hashem*, our village has refused to hire *khappers* to kidnap children. But as you both well know, many *kehillos* have succumbed to this dreadful practice and one never knows who is listening and who is nearby. You must not forget that there are enemies out there searching for you. Beware of Samoilov, and of army patrols. You are good *Yiddishe kinder*. I will pray for your safety with all of my heart and soul."

He then embraced them and blessed them.

The boys pushed the raft onto the quiet water. "We'll make it!" they called out to their well-wishers, with more assurance than they felt.

Chapter 5

REUVEN YAWNED AND blinked against the fiery slash of the setting sun. The dusk was resting heavily after an unusually pleasant day. He touched his lips to his new *siddur* before opening it to daven *maariv*. Though he knew his prayers by heart, he enjoyed seeing them printed before him.

The words of *Hashkiveinu* gripped him, refreshing his soul. Taking no notice of Archik's curious expression, he recited the prayer out loud and with great *kavanah*.

"Lay us down, Hashem, our God, in peace, and raise us up, our King, to good life and peace. Spread over us Your tabernacle of peace. Right us with good counsel before You. Save us speedily for the sake of Your name. Shield us, and remove from us every enemy, pestilence, sword, famine, and sorrow. Remove temptation from before and after us. Shelter us beneath the shadow of Your wings, for You are God, our guardian and deliverer;

God, our gracious and compassionate King, are You. Guard our going and coming for life and for peace, from now to eternity. Blessed be You, Hashem, who guards His people Israel eternally."

Reuven put his hands over his face, rocking back and forth until he concluded the evening prayers.

Archik, his own prayers long since completed, observed his companion with a troubled countenance. He leaned forward and placed his hand on Reuven's shoulder.

"My friend, we'll make it. You'll see," he murmured.

"With Hashem's help, Archik," Reuven sighed. "You are a good fellow, Archik, and I'm glad we're together." He paused, carefully weighing each word. "I only wish you would place more faith in Hashem," Reuven declared, his face flushed. "And it wouldn't hurt if you'd share some of your thoughts with me. It's," he paused, in search of the right words, "it's as if you don't trust me."

The silence was broken only by the waves lapping against their raft. At last Archik replied, "You must realize, Reuven, that by revealing my escape plan to you and asking you to join me, I placed my life in your hands. All I ask now is that you have a bit more patience with me and I promise that everything will be made clear in time. Until then," he said, his voice catching, "just be a good and trusting friend."

Reuven tried to make out his companion's face in the pale light. But Archik moved into the shadows and changed the subject.

"Tomorrow is Thursday and I think we should

head for shore. We need to restock our provisions. The map shows a village in this area, but it's at least a three-mile hike from the river, so let's try to get a good night's rest. And maybe tomorrow, we'll be lucky enough to be invited somewhere for Shabbos." Stifling a yawn, Archik leaned over and blew out the lamp. They drifted into the absolute stillness of the black night, and were soon asleep.

Early the next morning, they paddled to shore and trekked toward the village of Selezni, heading southwest through dewy pastures and flower-studded meadows, past pungent, freshly tilled soil and rainbows of butterflies. They walked at a good pace, arriving in Selezni in under an hour.

The village was a hodgepodge of ramshackle cottages and thatched, one-room huts. Some were surrounded by bare patches of land; others huddled together like so many crones. With no actual streets in sight, the lads made their way through the maze of rutted alleys. They trudged past the Jewish cem-etery, a tangle of tilted headstones, tall grass, and unkempt hedges. Some of the headstones, the boys could see, were relics from the Chmielnetzki pogroms.

Walking through the village, the boys were greeted by glares from the elderly Russian women gossiping on their stoops. The treeless alleys were filled with dust, and by the time they reached the village square, the air was redolent with the stale odors of day-old produce. Side by side, Jews and Russian peasants hawked their skimpy wares: onions, potatoes, parsnips, horseradish, and fish. Ducks and geese wandered underfoot; chickens shrieked and squawked for release from their cages. The square was alive with people arguing and haggling as kopeks and goods exchanged hands. The two lads ambled among the stalls, bargaining skillfully before buying the food they needed.

They also examined the men and women on the square in search of someone wearing Jewish garb; to their delight, there were indeed several Jewish vendors.

"I don't feel right about asking any of these poor people to put us up for Shabbos," Reuven said reflectively.

"Well, I suppose we could spend Shabbos under *HaKadosh Baruch Hu*'s own heaven, or maybe in the local shul," Archik replied with a shrug.

"Hey, look over there," Reuven called out, grabbing Archik's sleeve.

Without another word, the lads walked swiftly towards four Jewish children standing forlornly near a stall. As they approached, the oldest boy, barely bar mitzvah, shouted for the others to run off. They found themselves facing a youngster with a pinched face and tiny, crooked legs that held up a protruding belly. He remained glued in place, prepared for martyrdom.

"You're wasting your time with me. I don't have any money. Your buddies already stole everything we had," he warbled.

The young boy's words pierced the heart. Reuven held both palms up. "You're mistaken. We don't want anything from you, except maybe a place to spend Shabbos," he said, grinning and reverting to Yiddish. "Don't let our clothes fool you. We're *Yidden*."

The child's careworn face froze in amazement.

"Jews? But why are you dressed like *shkutzim*?" he asked, eyeing Archik suspiciously.

"Look, believe us, we're Jews. We are dressed this way..." Archik's voice trailed off. No need to reveal their true identity, he thought. "Let's just say that it's safer for us to travel like this."

"What's this about someone stealing your money?" Reuven interrupted.

The boy tossed his head sideways in the direction of three surly teenagers. "They took our money and now we haven't even a kopek left to buy food for Shabbos," he whimpered.

"What's your name?" Reuven asked kindly.

"Feivel Kamenetzky."

"You live nearby?"

"We live with the other Jews," he said, pointing toward the base of the hill, "at the edge of the village. My father was a blacksmith and his shed still stands near the house. He was killed two years ago in a pogrom," the boy whispered, wiping his tear-smudged face. "I'm the oldest of five children and I try to help as best as I can, earning a kopek or two doing chores here and there and cleaning the shul. My mother does laundry and sewing, earning just enough for black bread and onions. On Shabbos we sometimes have a small piece of fish. But now that my money was taken," he sobbed, "we won't have *any* food for Shabbos. Those <<MI%-2>>shkutzim! They pick on us 'cause they know we haven't got a father to defend us. They just came over and knocked me down and snatched my money away."

"Surely the other Jews won't let you go hungry," Reuven declared sympathetically.

The lad groaned. "This is a poor village, and everyone has his own *peckel* of *tzurris*. Besides, my mother is too proud to accept charity from her neighbors."

The boys glanced at each other. "Look, how many kopeks did you say they took from you?"

"Five."

Archik dug his hand into his jacket pocket and handed the startled boy the money. "Now hurry ahead and do your marketing. We'll make sure no one bothers you."

The youth stared down at his hand in amazement, then bounded off to the stalls, overcome by his unexpected good fortune.

"You've got something in mind?" Reuven inquired, observing Archik's expression.

"Come on, let's say hello to those brave thieves over there."

The two boys strolled over to the knot of bullies, their smiles open and friendly. "Hey, we just heard that you guys inherited some money from that Yid over there."

The thugs surveyed Reuven and Archik warily. "So what's it to you?" barked a stolid, sandy-haired boy with huge biceps and a vicious grin.

"We just thought that since we're strangers here, you'd like to share your 'inheritance.'"

The one who spoke up eyed Archik venomously. "You want trouble or something?"

"No, we just want you to give us the five kopeks as a sign of your hospitality."

Archik's last words were met with a punch to his ribs. He parried, dodging the next blow and meeting his opponent with a quick jab to the jaw, knocking him to the ground. Much to Archik's relief and surprise, the two other boys ran off, leaving their friend on his own. Seeing himself outfought and outnumbered, the brute threw the five kopeks in their direction, cursing them under his breath as he picked himself up from the dirt and raced after his cohorts.

"Well, we got back our five kopeks," Archik grinned.

"Are you crazy? We don't need the money. Now they'll be on the lookout for us."

Archik rubbed his jaw. "Well, they'll have a hard time finding us, won't they? Listen, Reuven, it wasn't the money, it was the principle. Maybe they'll leave the kids alone next time. They look like a pack of cowards anyway. Did you see them take off when their leader hit the ground? I never saw anyone run so fast," he chortled. "Now let's go look for a place to spend Shabbos, Reuven."

"I don't know. It's such a poor village. If we stay here, we'll be taking food from the mouths of the poor," Reuven asserted. "We can spend Shabbos outdoors and buy some food for that boy's family instead. What did he say his name was?"

"Kamenetzky."

"Well, this Thursday night the widow Kamenetzky and her children are in for a surprise."

Late that night the boys stealthily made their way

through Selezni, each carrying a sack filled with flour, onions, beets, potatoes, and fresh fruit. Except for the occasional wail of a child, the village slumbered.

As they approached the edge of the Jewish district, they scrutinized each house until a particularly ramshackle cottage loomed before them. The boys peered into the shed.

"What do you think, Archik?"

"Looks like a blacksmith's shed to me."

"Let's take a better look."

They inched their way in, the moon providing enough light for the young explorers to make out an anvil and a hammer. In the corner were bellows, and still hanging on rusty nails were horseshoes and corroded hinges.

"This is it," Reuven said hoarsely.

"Come on, then, let's get out of here. This place is eerie."

The boys crept toward the Kamenetzkys' wooden shack.

"Should we just leave the food and run?" Reuven whispered.

Archik frowned. "If we do, every animal for miles around will have a feast before sunrise."

Reuven sighed. "Maybe we can leave the sacks at the doorstep and then knock on the door. When we hear footsteps, we'll take off for the woods and no one will be the wiser."

Archik considered Reuven's plan, his face screwed

up in thought. "All right," he agreed.

The two boys heaved the sacks to the ground. Reuven tapped timidly and pressed his ear to the door. Hearing nothing, he knocked with greater urgency. Still no sound. Archik moved forward and pounded on the rickety door. Finally they heard the shuffle of feet and a woman's plaintive voice.

"Who is it?"

The boys dashed up the hill. Only when they were both out of breath did they turn around to observe the scene below. The widow Kamenetzky stood at the door, a ragged shawl about her shoulders, a lantern in her hand. Five shivering, barefoot children gathered about her. They could make out Feivel, who had bent down to open one of the sacks. In a moment he was jumping up and down in excitement.

The boys eyed each other, their grins stretching into smiles, and their smiles into whoops of joy.

"Did you see their faces?" Reuven asked, his eyes shining. "Do you think there's enough there to take care of them for a while?"

Archik shrugged. "I sure hope so, Reuven, because we've spent almost every kopek we had."

"Have no fear, Archik. Hashem will provide."

Chapter 6

TOO FAST, Reuven thought as he desperately wielded his oar to dodge a jagged rock that appeared out of the water. It had all happened too fast. One moment, it had been a cool, cloudy spring morning; the next, the sky had grown dark, thunder had rumbled louder and louder, and the river had begun a frighteningly rapid rise.

Only Reuven and Archik's skillful paddling kept the raft from being dashed against the giant cliffs that rose on both banks. Fiery bolts of lightning crackled across the black clouds and a bad-tempered wind hurled their raft across churning rapids. Finally, with a great, ugly roar, a wave engulfed the raft, depositing the startled boys in the murky water like so much driftwood.

Expelling mouthfuls of water, the lads repeatedly tried to seize the raft, but it seemed to fly past them on the violent water. Archik knew that if they could just gain some leverage, they might stop the raft from speeding away. Together, they made one last, determined effort: Archik dove under the raft and came up on the other side, and, as if on cue, each grabbed one side. They held on with every ounce of strength they could muster, letting the sturdy craft drag them along through the water.

When the storm finally passed and the raging waters simmered down, they dragged their wet, cold, and aching bodies onto the raft, too exhausted to do anything but thank God for being alive. They drifted for several hours, watching with weary amazement as the fickle weather cleared. As specks of white clouds dotted the now radiantly azure sky, they stirred from their fatigue, gazing out dreamily at the quiet landscape. Gone were the cliffs that had menaced them a few hours earlier. Now they stared at the miles of emerald farmland and the sprinklings of thatched cottages.

Their energy finally restored, the boys checked their provisions and found, with dismay, that most had been washed overboard. They had no choice but to ration their food. "If we don't find a village with some charitable Jewish families real soon, we'll starve," Reuven said gloomily.

"I suppose we have to pull into the next hamlet," Archik agreed. "And if there aren't any Jews around, maybe we can find some work. We just might earn enough for a meal or two."

"I don't feel comfortable in crowds," Reuven frowned, "especially crowds of *goyim*. I keep thinking about Rabbi Avigdor's warning. If it's not bandits and Samoilov, it's

Corporal Kolchak and the Russian army, or a bunch of bullies spoiling for a fight, or *khappers* looking to make a few rubles."

"Look, Reuven, be reasonable. We can't stay on this raft forever. We have to take our chances. You always remind me that Hashem is watching over us, and now you're the one who's losing faith!"

"*Chas vechallilah*, Archik. But you must admit that we have to be careful. We are surrounded by enemies like Kolchak and Samoilov who want nothing better than to destroy us."

Archik threw his hands in the air, shaking his head. "Enough of that, Reuven. Instead of mooning over our misery, let's daven *minchah*."

With the memory of the morning's storm still fresh, the boys prayers were heartfelt and long. The rest of the day went by uneventfully, and that night, despite their gnawing hunger, they slept peacefully.

It was the sound of gurgling water splashing over the sides of the raft that finally woke them. They washed, davened *shacharis*, and shared what was left of the boiled potatoes and raw beets, eating slowly in order to savor every morsel. Their next meal would be after *maariv*, when they would divide the leftover crusts of bread.

As if to make up for the day before, the sun soon blazed hot. The warmth combined with their hunger pangs to produce a kind of lethargy that lent itself to slumber. They spent much of their time halfheartedly shooing away the flies that gnawed at them, rousing themselves only when they needed to quench their thirst.

Stretching and squinting against the afternoon sunlight, Reuven suddenly spotted clusters of colorful tents and flags fluttering in the light breeze.

"Archik, Archik, take a look!" he said excitedly.

Archik shaded his eyes against the sun and peered into the distance. "A fair! We're going to the fair!" he yelped.

"Archik, I don't like that glint in your eye. Have you got a few ideas percolating in your head?"

Archik threw his head back in laughter. "Not yet, but something will come to me."

"That's just what I'm afraid of."

As the boys moored their raft, they realized that the festivities were much farther away than they had seemed from the river.

"This had better be some fair," Reuven grumbled as they raced inland.

The boys soon found themselves in the midst of a raucous crowd. Flags and banners fluttered overhead as peddlers touted their motley wares: trinkets, ribbons, sweets, pots and pans, crockery, hot sausages, breads and cakes, fruits, vegetables, and livestock. The air was thick with the smells of tobacco, spices, rotting fruit, and the unwashed tangle of humanity. The boys pushed through the throngs in search of Jewish vendors, but to no avail.

"What kind of work can we find here?" Reuven muttered, his stomach rumbling.

Archik ignored his friend, his eyes alight. How he enjoyed the unaccustomed excitement! The music, the noise, the crowds—all appealed to his brash and buoyant personality. He motioned for Reuven to follow as he elbowed his way in the direction of a knot of men and boys. Billowing in the breeze above them was a crudely scrawled banner announcing a horse race, with a purse of two gold rubles for the winner.

Nearby stood a stable filled with snorting, restless horses pawing the ground. Archik pulled himself onto the fence and pointed out which ones seemed built for speed and stamina.

Suddenly, they noticed a middle-aged peasant with a tangled black beard limping towards them. The man leered at the boys, and his very gait seemed menacing. Reuven paled. Had he recognized them from the description on the poster?

The man smiled at them, revealing rotting, tobacco-stained teeth, and clapped a thick, hairy hand on Archik's shoulder. "So you know something about horses, do you?" he asked, gazing intensely at Archik. "You know how to ride, boy?"

Archik nodded confidently. "I've been riding since I was a kid," he answered.

Again the peasant scrutinized him. "Tell you what, boy. How's about a deal? I've got me a good nag called Venture. But I hurt my leg in a fall this morning, and I won't be able to ride. You ride the horse, we share the purse fifty-fifty."

"Sure!" he exclaimed, jumping off the fence to shake the peasant's outstretched, clammy hand.

"You certain you can ride?" the peasant pressed,

giving him a sharp look. "I don't want anyone laming my horse."

"I've raced before," Archik said cockily.

"Good. So we've got a deal. My name is Pyotor Stepanovich. Yours?"

"Nikolai Vasilovich."

"Where you boys from?"

"Volchov," Archik replied, now almost believing it.

"Phew, that's far."

"Man's gotta eat."

"Yeah, times are hard. Not so great here, either, lads. Come along, I want you to meet Venture."

Archik sidled over to the handsome chestnut gelding and rubbed its nose. "Be a good fellow, Venture. We'll win, right?" he murmured encouragingly.

The horse whinnied.

"He likes you," Pyotor Stepanovich jabbed Archik playfully in the ribs. "I see that you have a way with horses."

Archik continued soothing the horse.

When Pyotor Stepanovich had stepped out of earshot, Reuven whispered, "Where'd you learn to ride?"

Archik grinned. "It's no great achievement, Reuven. My father was a milkman in Kozin and we had a team of horses and a wagon. When I was about six my father put me on a horse without a saddle and said, `Ride.' Once I got the hang of it, he had a saddle made for me. When I was a little older he sent me on errands, and when I was ten he even taught me how to handle the wagon and the team."

"But that's not racing."

Archik corrected his friend. "When he wasn't looking I'd race against the local *shkutzim*, and I usually won. Besides, what've we got to lose? There's nothing to worry about."

"I don't like the looks of that peasant. I have a feeling that if you lose, he'll be mighty angry," Reuven noted with a shudder.

"Who said anything about losing?"

Archik secured the saddle and mounted the towering steed, all the while whispering and patting the horse, which appeared jittery under its new rider.

There were eighteen contenders at the starting gate. Archik could feel their harsh eyes on him. Clearly the local peasants did not welcome an outsider entering the race, even on behalf of one of their own.

The track, if one could call it that, was nothing more than a cleared field. Yesterday's storm had apparently passed through this area as well, leaving the ground soft and muddy. Picking up speed would be difficult, Archik thought.

Suddenly a musket roared and the horses were off! Archik maintained an easy pace over the rough terrain, only urging Venture to gallop when they approached a small barrier, which the horse vaulted. Archik loosened his grip on the reins. Venture's hoofs pounded the sandy track, and they soon surged ahead of the others. Too late did Archik see two riders close in on him, their crops raised. One of them struck the horse's rump. Venture whinnied in protest, reared, and stamped his hoofs as he worked off his fury. The other riders were now ahead.

Archik held fast, managing to remain firmly in the saddle. He bent low and urgently whispered in Venture's ear, calming the shaken beast. Seconds later, he lightly kicked the horse, loosened the reins, and gave him his head. Although Venture was only a farm horse, he responded to Archik like a true thoroughbred. The course angled sharply, and Archik saw himself gaining on the leaders. He pleaded with the horse to make one last effort, his knees tightening about Venture's body. He raced the last yards with wild abandon, passing the finish line well before the others. There was no doubt who had won the race.

Venture reared and snorted noisily amid hurrahs from Pyotor Stepanovich's camp. Sweat poured down Archik's face and neck, spreading a dark stain across his back. As he dismounted, he was met by the peasant's hearty thump on his back. Archik's patron threw a blanket over his prize steed and offered him a sugar cube.

"I knew I had a winner in you, boy," Pyotor Stepanovich winked, handing Archik a gold ruble.

Archik wiped his face with the back of his damp hand and managed a triumphant smile. He caught his breath and walked over to a grinning Reuven.

"I thought for sure the horse would throw you, but you're a good horseman, Archik," he marveled, flinging his arm about Archik's shoulders. "Now that we've got some money, let's go buy some provisions. I'm famished."

Archik glanced about uneasily. "Never mind the food, let's get out of here as fast as we can."

"What's the matter?"

"Never mind, let's just get out of here."

Once they got past the crowds, they began running. Reuven was not quite sure why they were rushing away from the fair, but he valued his friend's instincts and kept pace with him. Reuven soon saw that Archik's intuition had proved right. No sooner had they left the fairgrounds than Pyotor Stepanovich and five of his cronies had them surrounded. The ringleader waddled toward them, his eyes gleaming.

"Why are you fine lads leaving us so soon?" he said as he grabbed Archik's shoulder. "You're not being a good sport, laddie, leaving in such a hurry without even showing your gratitude. We gave you a gold ruble, and we sure figured you'd treat us to a few rounds of ale."

Archik drew away from the peasant.

"We don't appreciate outsiders coming here and taking what's rightly ours," Pyotor Stepanovich growled.

"I won that race fair and square, and you were the one who suggested we share the purse."

"Did I? Why would I want to share my winnings with you?" the man grunted, his finger jabbing Archik's thin shoulder.

The other men laughed raucously as the two boys stood forlornly before them.

"Give him the money and let's get out of here," Reuven muttered, his eye catching the glint of their knives.

Archik swallowed hard and met the man's gaze.

"All right, you win. You can have your ruble."

Just as Archik was about to relinquish the coin, the sound of hoofbeats drew everyone's attention. Astride a large, brown horse sat a rider, his rifle cocked and aimed at them. Attached to his horse were two yearlings, a beautiful filly and a frisky colt. The man loomed over them like a giant, his face ruddy, a huge, black mustache curled over his lip and up the sides of his face, and his jet-black hair slicked straight back, revealing a strong Roman nose. He motioned angrily at the two boys.

"Count Kropotkin has been looking for you. I've come to fetch you home," he bellowed, indicating that they untie the horses and mount.

The five peasants fell to their knees, their caps doffed.

"There's been a mistake," Pyotor Stepanovich stuttered. "We're just having some sport with the lads, nothing serious. We swear by all that is holy. And besides, they never told us they were related to the Count."

"You are nothing but a bunch of mangy dogs," the rider grunted. "Nikolai Vasilovich won that race for you fair and square, you scurvy mongrel, and now you want to take his winnings. The Count will hear of this, you can be sure," he shouted, his face red with rage. The five peasants remained in their kneeling position as the boys and their rescuer raced off toward the river, Reuven and Archik exchanging incredulous glances.

"Sir," Reuven faltered as they reached the riverside, "how did you know who we were?"

The man dismounted and helped the boys to the ground. “My name is Ivan Petrovich and I’m in charge of the Count’s stables. I saw Stefan bring you boys to the Count’s summer home, and he later told us all about the rescue of our beloved little Nikolai. Well,” he said, scratching his hairy ear, “seems to me it was Providence that brought me here today. The Count heard there was some fine horseflesh in these parts and he sent me to see what I could find for our stables. After I picked up these two magnificent specimens, and struck a good bargain to boot, I figured I’d treat myself to a few hours at the fair.

“No sooner did I arrive than I heard a horse race was being run. I went to have a look, and whom do I see in the saddle but our little Nikolai’s lifesaver. You looked good in the saddle and I figured you for a winner,” he chuckled, “so I placed a small bet on the side. You didn’t disappoint me, lad, and I even made a few kopeks. I’m proud of you, young man. You ran a good and fair race. I saw how those thugs tried to dismount you, but you sure surprised them,” he chortled, winking broadly. “I figured I would have a good tale to tell Stefan and Nadia as well as the Count.

“But when I heard the men grousing about having to share the purse with foreigners, I knew you boys were in for trouble. So I figured I’d follow you and give them a scare,” he laughed. “They won’t sleep for a few nights, I guarantee you that. The truth is, I should have blown their heads off,” he muttered under his breath, his expression darkening. “Anyway, let it be a lesson to you: this world is filled with evil men and you can’t be too trusting.

“Another word of warning: the army is still looking

for you. A certain Corporal Kolchak returned to the Count's *dacha* weeks after you left and the cook overheard one of the stablemen say that you two had been there. I have a feeling they are hot on your trail, so be careful," he warned. "You're good boys and deserve better. Now climb aboard your raft and I'll help you push off. And remember to keep out of the path of those wolves," he stressed, his eyes darting back in the direction of the fair. He dug his hand in his pocket and handed a startled Archik twenty-five kopeks. "Part of the winnings," he said, clapping Archik's shoulder.

Archik raised his hand in refusal.

"You deserve it for putting up with those thugs," the peasant admonished. "Now off you go, and watch your step."

"We are grateful to you, Ivan Petrovich. God Himself was watching over us," Reuven observed. "Please send our best wishes to the Count and his family and tell him that we are indebted to him and his good-hearted servants."

"My master will be delighted to hear that you are both well. Now go with God, my good lads," he called out as they pulled away from the shore.

Archik fingered the pouch around his neck, his expression pensive.

"What are you thinking, Archik?"

"Well," he drawled, "the first thing we'll do tomorrow is pull in for supplies, and second...."

Reuven's eyes brightened. "And second, Archik, since we have so much to be grateful for, we will give part of your winnings to *tzedakah*."

Chapter 7

THE RAYS OF the early summer sun reflected off the quiet surface of the river. The boys stretched their cramped bodies and yawned noisily, then washed and davened. Morning's mist soon evaporated to reveal acres of purple-flowered alfalfa on the bank. Beyond that, squatting alone, stood a thatched cottage, smoke curling from its chimney.

Reuven examined the jug they used to collect rainwater. There was just enough for one good gulp. He licked his parched lips.

"We'll each take one sip," Reuven suggested, urging Archik to drink first.

Archik let the water trickle slowly into his mouth and then swished it about and handed the jug back to Reuven. "We'll have to pull in here and see what we can buy from those peasants, and refill our jug from their well," Archik said, peering in the direction of the cottage.

Reuven looked worried. The news that Kolchak was still on their trail had left him shaken.

"Just leave it to me, Reuven."

Both knew they had no choice. Either they would attempt to obtain food from whatever source was available, or they would starve. Archik's stomach rumbled, reminding him that his last meal had consisted of one crust of bread eaten as they had drifted away from the fairgrounds.

The shore offered scant cover for their raft, but the hungry boys did not have the energy to care. They covered the raft with a few large branches and then began what they had estimated would be a good mile-long trek to the house in the distance. The hot sun blazed down as they trudged along a winding dirt road toward the thatched cottage.

As they approached, a bird flew off the roof, no doubt heading for a cooler perch. Two dogs greeted them, but even they seemed exhausted by the heat. One forlorn mutt, its ribs poking through its mangy coat, ran about in mad circles in search of its tail. The other, a larger hound, seemed too lethargic to do more than stand on its haunches, snarling and showing its canines.

Several chickens waddled about, clucking and pecking the ground. Three goats sauntered past, eyeing them with disinterest, hunting for something munchable. Near a trough stood a rickety fence, penning in a sow and her piglets. A shed served as a barn, and a weary, swaybacked horse swished his tail against the flies.

Several cows could be seen grazing contentedly in the distant pasture. For a moment it appeared as if there was no human life about.

The illusion was shattered when a woman stepped out from the cottage, her head wrapped in a faded scarf, her face weathered. A barefoot boy of about five, dressed in clean but threadbare clothes, clutched her skirt, and his younger sister, no more than three, held fast to the boy's arm. The girl stepped toward them, extending a pudgy hand, as if to touch them. Archik and Reuven exchanged looks. The little girl was blind.

The woman had a pleasant, open face. She offered a modest grin as she wiped her work-reddened hands on a smudged apron.

"Well, what brings you two lads here?" she inquired curiously. And then, studying them more astutely, she shook her head. "You two must be a long way from home, and seems to me you haven't had a square meal in some time."

"We'd appreciate some water, ma'am, and if it's possible we would like to buy some food," Archik replied softly.

The woman threw her hands in the air. "You want to buy food? How will you pay for it? We have no need for farmhands, thank the good Lord. I have three healthy sons out in the fields with their father. But I can spare a meal if you'll mend that over there," she said, pointing toward the fence.

Reuven stepped forward, his eyes lowered. "We can pay with money, ma'am. But we will also gladly mend the fence."

"Well, bless my heart, two good boys," she marveled, shooing away the chickens that now clucked about her. "You can wash up if you like," she urged, pointing to the cistern behind the house. "And then I'll make you some food and we'll talk about what we have to sell."

"Ma'am," Reuven said quietly, "we don't wish to bother you. There is no need to prepare a meal for us, though we would appreciate something to drink, and water to fill our jug. Then we will mend the fence and be off."

The woman drew back, her expression suspicious. "Are you boys fugitives? Are you running from the police?"

Reuven flushed. "No, no," he stammered, "we're from Volchov and we're looking for work."

The woman shoved her hands into her apron, a compassionate smile softening her face. "So you're the boys from Volchov? Well, the Lord truly works in strange ways."

Reuven glanced nervously at Archik. "I beg your pardon, ma'am?"

"My sister Nadia works for Count Kropotkin. She visited me just a month ago and told me all about the boys from Volchov who saved the future Count. Come, lads," she laughed, throwing her head back, "you have nothing to fear from us. Now I insist that you share something with us. Some hard- boiled eggs at least. Those you'll eat, won't you?"

Reuven gave her a sharp, questioning look.

The woman smiled. "When I was a young girl, I lived in a village where we had some Jewish families. I did housework for them. So," she chuckled, "I know what you boys can and can't eat. Now if you will be patient, I will see to getting some fresh eggs." She looked up at the sun, shading her eyes against its glare. "My husband, Alexei, will be here soon and we can have our morning meal together. My boys eat in the fields in the summer, so no one will know about your visit," she said reassuringly. "But I must warn you, a search party passed through here two days ago. They are offering a handsome reward for you boys." Her face darkened. "But no need to worry. You are safe here for the moment," she promised them. "Ah, yes," she added as an afterthought, "my name is Maria Ivanovna."

Moments later they saw a man approaching. Maria Ivanovna rushed from the cottage and headed toward him. Soon the two were deep in earnest discussion.

The boys exchanged uneasy glances. "Maybe we should make a run for it," Archik said.

"How far could we get?" Reuven reasoned.

"What do you think? Can we trust her?"

Reuven shrugged.

Alexei Fydorovich barely greeted his guests. He was short and stocky, with a receding hairline and strong, callused hands that matched his hard-muscled body. They ate their meager meal in silence.

"We are a poor family," Alexei Fydorovich began what appeared to be the negotiations, "but I can spare some potatoes, onions, and beets."

“Thank you. That will be fine,” Archik said, digging into his pocket and pulling out twenty-five kopeks. “Will this be enough?”

The peasant eyed the money greedily. “We need money for our child,” he said gruffly, glancing toward his daughter. “Irina was not born blind. She came down with a fever a few months ago. We thought for sure we would lose her. We even called in the *feldsher*.”

The boys knew only too well that summoning a *feldsher*, a healer who served the villagers, indicated a life-threatening ailment.

“Alas, the *feldsher* was helpless,” he sighed. “He said something about the nerves of our Irina’s eyes being damaged, and about her needing a specialist to help her. The longer we wait, the less chance our little girl has to regain her sight. Life is bitter enough with eyes,” he groaned. “What chance does our daughter have without them?”

“How much money do you need for such an examination?” Reuven asked, gazing in pity at the child now groping her way about the cottage.

“My wife’s sister, a good woman, gave us her life savings of five rubles, and the good Count added another five to her purse. We just need a little more to travel to an eye specialist in Moscow.”

Archik opened the pouch about his neck. “Alexei Fydorovich, please take this gold ruble. I won it honestly, and,” he said, swallowing hard, “my friend and I want you to have it.”

Maria Ivanovna gasped. She covered her face with

her hands and sobbed for a few moments. She then turned to the boys. "It is as I said: the good Lord has directed you to our humble home. May your Jewish God bless you and keep you safe," she said, unable to contain her sobs once again.

Later that day, as Alexei loaded his wagon with the supplies the lads needed, Maria Ivanovna took them aside. "I must tell you the truth. My husband was ready to turn you both in for the ransom. He's not a bad man, but we needed the money so desperately, and you are fugitives, after all. But I begged him to wait and think it over. You did save the Count's son. And somehow I felt that the good Lord had sent you to us. I was right. Now you have nothing to fear. Your generosity has softened my husband's heart."

In fact, Alexei gave them more provisions than they had bargained for. They loaded the sacks onto their raft, the peasant's grateful generosity leaving them little extra room on board. Before saying their farewells, the peasant embraced them both.

"God bless you and keep you safe. You will always be in our prayers, this I promise you."

As they were about to pull away, Reuven turned to Archik. "What made you give them that ruble?"

"It's hard to say exactly. I just felt sorry for the little girl. She seemed so helpless."

"Well, whatever it was that made you offer the money also saved our lives."

They exchanged knowing smiles and then davened *minchah*. As they swayed to and fro, they thanked the

Ribono shel olam once again for watching over them.

The raft began drifting away when a boy about their age raced toward them, calling out, "Hey there, wait up!"

The lad was barefoot, his clothing nothing more than a collection of patches and tatters. He had the face of a typical Russian peasant, with unwashed, straw-blond hair falling about his shoulders. They paddled back to shore grudgingly, not wanting to arouse the boy's suspicions.

The peasant smiled broadly and extended a grubby hand. "Where you guys heading?"

"Wherever there's work," Archik replied, not eager to have him join them.

"Can I hitch a ride?"

"We haven't got much room."

"That's okay. I don't take up much space. Besides, just to the next village. Can't be that far."

"All right," Archik sighed, unable to think of a reason to refuse. He helped the boy onto the crowded raft and pushed off onto the river.

"My name's Grigor."

They introduced themselves.

"You guys run away from home?"

"Nah, just looking for work. And you?" Archik asked, anxious to change the subject.

"I ran away from home. My father beat me all the time, and we ain't never had any food anyway, so I figured, can't do worse on my own." He dug his hand into his bag. "Hey, fellows, want to see what I got?"

The two shrugged indifferently.

Grigor pulled out a pair of tefillin!

The blood drained from their faces.

"What's that?" Archik spluttered, trying to hide his shock.

"I stole it from my dad. He said it was a good-luck amulet the *zhids* use. So I figured I needed it more than he did."

"How does it work?" Reuven asked evenly.

"My poppa said you wrap it around your arm, something like this, and you put this little hat on your head," Grigor explained, "and then you mutter something."

Archik laughed. "Your dad was sure taken in."

The boy looked up sourly. "Whadya mean?"

"My poppa knew lots of *zhids* and they told him the charm doesn't work unless you got two, one for each arm. If not, it's worth nothin'."

The boy examined the tefillin, turning them over several times as if in search of some answer. He scratched his pimply chin and then threw the tefillin across the raft. Fortunately, his aim was poor and the tefillin landed between the potato sacks instead of dropping into the river. "Just like my poppa. Nothin' he does is right," he spat out.

No sooner had they dropped off Grigor than they lovingly retrieved the cast-off tefillin.

"We'll have them checked by a *sofer* as soon as we get to a Jewish village," Reuven exclaimed, his eyes shining with delight. He then laughed heartily. "That was brilliant, Archik. You really are a clever fellow. `One for each arm,'" he chuckled. "Now that's quick thinking."

Archik blushed at Reuven's effusive praise. He leaned back on one of the sacks, a satisfied smile surfacing. "Well, who would have imagined that a *shaigetz*, of all people, would be a bearer of tefillin?"

Chapter 8

IN THE SOFT, hazy twilight of early August, Reuven and Archik pulled into what appeared to be a welcoming shore. The recent rains had left behind lush vegetation, and they had no difficulty finding cover for their raft. Beyond the shore lay a dark woodland. At the rim of the forest, ancient trees elbowed their way toward the sunlight, their branches groaning with heavy leaves. Curiosity drew the boys into a dank, fetid world of ferns, mold, creeping vines, and mushrooms growing wild under massive tree trunks. Reuven and Archik giggled as they skidded along the slippery carpets of moss and algae.

Heading back to the riverbank, Archik carefully unfolded his precious map and drew his finger across their escape route.

So far his judgment had not been faulty, he thought happily. If his calculations proved correct, they should reach their destination before the river froze over.

"I think we're making good time," Archik observed, a triumphant smile stealing across his aristocratic face. He refolded the map and placed it in the oilskin bag kept snugly under his shirt.

The two then began scavenging for dry kindling. Gathering whatever looked combustible, they finally coaxed a sputtering flame out of the sticks and leaves, just enough of a fire to boil water for tea and cook up a stew of potatoes, beets, and onions for their evening meal.

Night crept across the heavens. The boys davened and then curled up on the ground, the sound of crickets and the floral-scented air of the midsummer night lulling them off to sleep.

And then Reuven was drawn back to wakefulness. Something seemed wrong. He listened intently to the tranquil sounds of the night. Once again he attempted to sleep, but a strange sense of foreboding refused to leave him. Suddenly he heard the snap of twigs. Fear fingered every bone in his body. Was it his imagination playing tricks on him? Then he heard a shushing sound accompanied by muffled voices. He rolled over and prodded Archik awake. His friend was about to register a noisy protest when the distant voices grew closer and more distinct. They looked at each other in the strained silence of growing panic. The two jumped to their feet, and doused the fire's glowing embers before darting into the woods. They crouched under a large maple, hoping not to be seen. But in minutes, a halo of lantern light revealed a ring of evil faces.

"Is it Kolchak?" Reuven gasped.

"Shh," whispered Archik.

It wasn't long before the men found the two boys cowering beneath the tree. With one of the men holding the lantern close, the leader leaned over and examined their faces. To their horror, the boys saw the wicked visage of Samoilov the bandit! He lifted Archik's chin with a dirt-encrusted hand, his eyes filled with venom.

"So it's you!" he growled. "Did you really think you'd escape Samoilov's vengeance? Tomorrow you will see what becomes of those who cross me!"

The bandits surrounded the terrified boys, their ominous grins betraying their sadistic intent. Samoilov ordered them to be trussed together like lambs made ready for a spit. Neither had the heart to speak. With the *Shema* on their lips, they closed their eyes and grimly awaited the next day.

The night turned into a gray dawn. Samoilov was the first to open his vodka-glazed eyes. He pulled his thickset body from the ground, cleared his throat raucously, and deposited a wad of spittle at the boys' feet, wiping his thick lips with the back of his hand. The other bandits woke one at a time, each following Samoilov's lead. Their heads lowered, Reuven and Archik began to daven through dry lips. The men muttered among themselves, kicking the boys from time to time, to the fettered prisoners' misery.

The fire was rekindled and the men gorged themselves on gruel and bread. Only then did Samoilov fix his murderous gaze on his two captives.

"So you really thought you'd put one over on Samoilov, heh?" he growled, eyeing them with increasing enmity. "The *zhids* must have paid you plenty for your treachery. And here I was goin' to be like a father to you, takin' care of you, sharin' our booty with you.... But no, you go to the *zhids* to fill your pockets. We ain't good enough, is that it?"

He waddled toward his men, glowering at them.

"You filthy curs, just remember what treachery will get you. If you get any funny ideas in your heads, remember what happened to these two, who weren't satisfied with joining Samoilov. You're gonna see Samoilov's judgment and Samoilov's punishment. And let that be a lesson to any of you," he growled, staring at his men, "to anyone who doublecrosses me," he shouted, scraping his finger across his throat. His face was livid. "Death is too good for them, " he said with passion. "But death it will be. Not a nice, easy death, oh no, not for anyone who crosses me. First we'll have a bit of sport," he cackled as the others licked their lips in expectation.

The tightly bound boys were dragged and tethered to two snorting horses. Reuven gazed across at Archik helplessly, his eyes brimming with tears. "Be brave, my friend. Put your trust in *HaKadosh* Baruch Hu," he whispered. "You must have faith that the Almighty will be at our side. Don't lose faith, don't give up!" he cried out as the horses leaped forward to the crack of the whip. Both boys screamed,<<MI%-2>> "Shema Yisrael!" as the horses raced across the field, dragging Reuven and Archik over the deeply rutted terrain. The pebbles tore at their flesh. Back and forth the horses charged, the bandits cheering them on, their screams and shouts reaching insane fury. The circus of cruelty ended only when Samoilov and his gang were certain the boys were no longer conscious.

"What did they scream?" one bandit asked as he spit a thick wad of tobacco to the ground.

The others shrugged as they untied their limp victims.

"When do we kill them?" one henchman croaked.

"When we finish having our fun," snorted another.

Samoilov doused the boys with water but, to his dismay, the two responded with unconscious groans.

Their disappointment great, the bandits amused themselves by ransacking the boys' belongings.

"Hey, what's this stuff?" one thug shouted as he drew out their tefillin and *siddurim*. He held them at arm's length as if fearful of infection, his face curdling in disgust. Just as he was about to consign them to the fire, Samoilov rushed over and grabbed them from his hands. He examined the tefillin carefully, then leafed through the *siddurim*, his brow furrowing as he searched his mind for some distant memory. After a few moments of thought, a cryptic smile emerged from beneath a stubbly beard. He struck his brow with the flat of his hands. "Well, I'll be!" he exclaimed. "We've got ourselves two Jew boys."

"*Zhids*?"

"Yeah," he growled with growing pleasure, a plan germinating in his wily head. "Yeah, my good fellows, we sure got ourselves real treasure. Now listen carefully. I'm leaving here and I'll be gone for a day or two. When I get back, I want those two *zhids* alive. Clean them up and feed them, you got that? Whatever you do, don't let them croak on us. They gotta stay alive. Anything happens to them and you'll all be nothin' more than dog meat," he warned.

The bandits stared at Samoilov, puzzled. Had their leader gone crazy?

"They're *zhids*. Why not kill them and be rid of the scurvy dogs?" one bandit called out malevolently.

"Because, you numbskull, I've got a better plan for these two."

"A better plan? What can be better than having some fun with the scum and then cutting their Jew throats?" another demanded with a bloodthirsty leer.

Samoilov stood with his legs apart, one hand resting on his hip. "You fools, ain't you got no imagination? That's the difference between you and me, and that's why I'm the boss and you're just a bunch of empty-headed louts. Without me you'd all starve," he shouted, gesticulating angrily. "These boys mean rubles, gold rubles. All we have to do is tell the Jews we got two Jew boys as prisoners, and you'll see, our pockets will be filled with ransom. Real money. Jew money," he said, licking his lips in anticipation. "So you bloodthirsty thugs had better not kill the geese that will lay our golden eggs, heh? Just remember, keep your filthy paws off them. And make sure they are alive and well by the time I return," he warned.

Samoilov mounted his horse, spurring it cruelly,

and headed swiftly to the nearby town of Ulla.

When consciousness returned, every inch of Reuven's body throbbed with searing pain. He gazed down at Archik, who was still unconscious, and prayed fervently for his friend to survive.

"Archik," he whispered, "Archik, wake up, wake up! You must wake up. Please, wake up, I beg you."

Archik moaned and moved slightly. Though they were both tied securely to a tree, Reuven strained against the ropes and managed to reach out and touch his friend.

Archik's eyes fluttered open. He saw Reuven through a haze of agony. Strangely enough, it was the pain that assured him that he was still alive. Reuven's face seemed to float before him. He tried to focus his eyes but to no avail. He wanted to speak, to call out, but nothing emerged. If not for Reuven, he thought as waves of pain swept over him, he would have succumbed without resistance. Hammers now pounded in his head and still he could not stop thinking about Reuven: good old reliable Reuven, a bit too pious and phlegmatic for his taste, but someone you could count on. It was Reuven who had the real mettle; it was Reuven who had not flinched in the face of death. Archik could only marvel at Reuven's strength, which he knew sprung from his deep faith in Hashem. Reuven had faced death with fortitude. Now, with all his heart, Archik wanted to reach out to his friend, to share his feelings with him. "Reuven, Reuven," he rasped before drifting back into unconsciousness.

In that deep, velvet darkness, he was once again

home in Kozin, seated on the milk wagon alongside his father, proud to assist him on his milk route; proud when his father called him, "my little *yingeleh*." He saw himself astride his father's sturdiest mare, Mooky, learning to handle the horse with confidence. "You must sit well. That's it," his father instructed. "One day you will be able to run errands for me all the way to Kiev." And then his father patted him on the shoulder, a smile cutting through his thick, curly beard. "Archik, your momma and I are proud of you. Reb Yehoshua tells us that you have a fine grasp of the Chumash."

Other memories, other scenes. Ugly memories of being harassed and beaten by the *shkutzim* and by some of his own classmates. "Dirty gypsy; foundling; adopted." His father begged him to ignore these words, though he never explained what they meant, or why some ostracized him. As he grew older and learned what these names meant, he turned to his father for answers. But his father was evasive: "Life is not easy, my son. You must learn to ignore what they say. If you have faith in Hashem, in time they will tire of their sport and leave you in peace." He tried to follow his father's instructions, but the jibes never stopped, and more often than not he responded with his fists. His sisters and mother would sigh and shake their heads when he came home bloodied. Their gentle ministrations eased the pain of his wounds, but not even their love could lessen the bitterness of rejection. For many years questions remained unanswered; and when at last the answers came, it was too late, too late to matter.

A bucket of ice water brought Archik back to the present. His hands had been untied. The world slowly came into focus. He looked down at his rope-scarred wrists, trying to rub away the numbness. Reuven sat nearby, nibbling on a chunk of stale bread that he had dunked into a tumbler of tea. Archik extended a quivering hand, trying to get his attention. Reuven turned his way, his eyes wide in wonder.

"Archik, you're awake! *Baruch Hashem!*" he cried out. "I was so afraid..." the words trailed off.

Archik smiled wanly in return. "I'm not that easily gotten rid of, my friend."

Reuven broke off a piece of bread and dunked it into the lukewarm tea, softening it enough to make it edible. He then placed the bread in his friend's trembling hand. "Please try to eat. You need the strength."

Archik waved his hand in refusal.

"Please. I've had my fill, believe me."

Archik glanced at the bandits sitting not far from them. Reuven understood his unvoiced fear.

"Don't worry, Archik, Hashem is looking out for us. I heard them talking. It seems that Samoilov wants us alive—he's gone to a nearby Jewish town to demand a ransom."

The thieves threw menacing looks their way. Fear of their leader may have kept them in check, but not a minute passed without verbal abuse. And whenever Ivan Groanchik, Samoilov's second in command, was not looking, one or two would come by and surreptitiously kick the boys in their already bruised ribs.

"How long will this go on?" Archik appealed to his

friend.

"Until Samoilov gets back with a promise of ransom."

"Do you think we'll be ransomed, Reuven?"

Reuven stirred. "With Hashem's help. You know, Archik, ransoming Jewish prisoners is a great mitzvah." Reuven's throat contracted. "You must have great faith in Hashem, my friend. Only *HaKadosh* Baruch Hu can help us now, and we must not falter."

Archik nodded, not looking up. "Reuven," he whispered, still staring at the hard ground, "I confess that I lack your *bitachon*. It isn't that I don't believe in Hashem, *chas vechallilah*, but..." he hesitated, and then with a toss of the head added, "I just can't put my feelings into words."

"Archik, I understand. And I only wish I could help strengthen you."

Archik looked up sharply. "But Reuven, don't you see that you have already?"

Reuven's face took on a meditative cast. And then with a deep sigh, he said, "Archik, let's daven together. We know the words by heart. Let's now engrave them into our hearts."

The synagogue of Ulla was built of solid stone, a remnant of a more prosperous time for the town's Jews. Within, a brass chandelier cast shadows upon the worried, grim faces of Ulla's communal leaders. Seated around a walnut table in the synagogue study hall, the officers of the local *kehillah* looked grim.

It was the head of the *kehillah*, Reb Hershel Grossman, who opened the meeting. A man of means, with a round, sunny face and a full, rust-brown beard cascading down his chest, Reb Grossman was generally affable. But not on this unhappy day. For the first time in years, he did not caress the shining brass chain that rose over his rotund form, or glance at the gold timepiece he would usually draw out of his pocket and click open and shut several times an hour. The members of the *kehillah* suffered his little vanities with good humor since Hershel Grossman was also a charitable man who could be counted on to help the widow and the orphan, and to support many Torah scholars.

"Members of the *kehillah*," he said, his voice heavy with emotion, "many of you may already know why we are gathered here today." He removed a white linen handkerchief and wiped the beads of perspiration from his brow. "Early this morning, we had the misfortune of having a most unwelcome visitor here in our midst."

The room grew hushed. The members of the *kehillah* leaned forward.

"Our good Rabbi Yecheskel Marinberg and I were returning home after *shacharis* when the rabbi graciously invited me to his home for a glass of tea. No sooner were we seated and enjoying the rebbetzin's delicious strudel when there was a fearful pounding on the door.

"With both the servant and the rebbetzin out at the market, the rabbi rushed to the door himself, and was shocked to see the notorious anti-Semite, Samoilov, standing before him."

A gasp shook the room.

"The insolent man pushed past our esteemed rabbi and ensconced himself in an easy chair, ordering the rabbi to pour him a glass of tea. Of course, I would not hear of such a thing," he assured the assembled, "and I would have protested had the man not appeared so...so threatening," he stammered uncomfortably. "There was little choice but to serve the beast myself."

Even those who had heard earlier of Samoilov's morning visit shook their heads in dismay, their faces drawn with sadness.

Again mopping his brow, the head of the *kehillah* continued.

"What can I tell you, my good friends and neighbors, but that this animal on two feet, who had forced his way into our beloved rabbi's home, then had the chutzpah to tell us he was holding two Jewish children for ransom," he groaned. "And as proof, he brought their tefillin. This villain then informed us of his plan to wreak terrible vengeance on these two innocents because they had foiled his pogrom in Zabori. He will only spare their lives if we come up with a large ransom," he sighed. "Seeing that monster seated before me, I had no doubt that if we do not give him the money, he will carry out his threat," he muttered hoarsely. "And now these children's lives are in our hands!"

"This could be some kind of a trick," Shmuel Klotz pointed out.

"Reb Shmuel, the rabbi and I were well aware that he could have found the tefillin elsewhere. So we made it very clear that no ransom would be paid until we see the boys alive and well and in our hands."

"Maybe we should call the police?" Duvid Applebaum called out.

"The police," Hershel Grossman said solemnly, "are no better than Samoilov."

"So what does the fiend want?" Feivish Hazelkorn asked quietly.

"As I said, it was a huge sum."

"How much?" Yoel Fishman exclaimed, growing irritated with Reb Hershel's oratory.

"Five hundred rubles."

The room reverberated in a unanimous outcry. "Five hundred rubles! How much time do we have to raise this...Gthis outrageous sum?" Duvid Applebaum spluttered.

"Until Thursday," Hershel Grossman replied.

"But that's impossible," Applebaum pleaded. "After paying outrageous taxes and bribing every petty official for the right to breathe the air, we have virtually nothing left for our families! Where can we ever get such a sum?"

"Samoilov had no interest whatsoever in our economic difficulties, I can assure you," Hershel Grossman shot back sharply. "Believe me, the rabbi and I tried our best to suggest a more reasonable sum of money, Reb Duvid. Now let us not dicker. This is a clear case of *pidyon shevuyim*, the mitzvah of ransoming captives."

"And how do you suggest we raise this kind of money so quickly, Hershel? Even if we each pledge forty or fifty rubles, we will still be short of the sum," Yoel Fishman stated matter-of-factly.

Velvel Kaminsky jumped to his feet. "This is nonsense. I make just enough to feed and clothe my family. Should I leave my wife and children destitute to ransom other Jewish children? What you ask is impossible," he fumed.

Rabbi Yecheskel rose, his palms raised in a conciliatory gesture. "My dear friends, let us not raise our voices in anger. We Jews have faced greater dangers before and we have prevailed. Now we have an important mitzvah to fulfill and we will fulfill it. We have no choice but to ransom our brethren in distress and this we shall do. No one is forced to give any specific amount, but I beg you, open your hearts. We cannot let the *sonei Yisrael* prevail."

Reb Hershel Grossman jumped to his feet. "Rabbi, I will pledge fifty rubles for the sake of ransoming these poor children."

After further discussion, two hundred rubles was raised, still a far cry from the five hundred demanded by Samoilov.

"Maybe we should once again try to negotiate with this Samoilov. Maybe he will be reasonable and accept two hundred rubles for the boys?" Yoel Fishman said hopefully.

The rabbi shook his head. "I tried to persuade the man. I explained the impossibility of his demands, but he remained adamant." The rabbi left the table to pace the room, his fingers nervously combing his silver-streaked beard. Suddenly, he stopped near the head of the table and seized Hershel Grossman's arm with a trembling hand. "There just may be a way to raise the ransom."

All eyes turned in his direction.

"Reb Gershom Lader usually visits our town at the beginning of August. If I am not mistaken, he should be arriving here within days. His visit just may be the answer to our prayers."

"Dear rabbi, what can this itinerant peddler do for us?" Duvid Applebaum inquired dryly. "He doesn't strike me as a man of substance."

"You are right, Reb Duvid, but though Reb Gershom is only a peddler by profession, he has many influential and, I might add, wealthy friends. These contacts may prove useful to us. If he can approach some of these people...need I say more?"

What Rabbi Marinberg was not at liberty to tell the members of the *kehillah* was that his old friend Gershom Lader was far more than a simple peddler, although that was how he had started out in life. Fate and Gershom Lader's integrity combined to draw him into another world, and many years ago he had become a courier on behalf of the far-flung Russian Jewish communities.

Reb Hershel himself went out to greet Reb Gershom as he clambered into Ulla that very afternoon with his wagon filled with farm implements. "Reb Gershom," he wailed, "a tragedy has befallen our community!"

Gershom listened with speechless indignation as Reb Hershel recounted the events of the day. By the time he reached the rabbi's house, the peddler had been apprised of the entire situation, and his keen mind was already at work.

Rabbi Marinberg greeted his friend joyfully and led him to his study, where Gershom eased his large, muscular frame into an easy chair. As he munched on the sponge cake the rebbetzin had baked especially for him, the rabbi explained the impossibility of ever amassing so much money in so little time. "I fear the boys are doomed!" the rabbi moaned.

Gershom Lader rose, heaving a heavy sigh. He stroked his beard as he paced the floor. "Rabbi, let me see what I can do. I can't promise miracles, but I will do my best."

Reb Gershom left his wagon full of wares behind, borrowing a sturdy young stallion for the long, arduous journey ahead. He planned to make his way to Sumilino, to the summer residence of the great philanthropist Baron Isaac Anshel Rothenberg.

Gershom had met Itzik Rothenberg on one of his earliest trips to Kreslavka, Latvia. At the time, they were both young married men and they took an immediate liking to one another despite the fact that Itzik came from a relatively wealthy home. Itzik, who had just completed his studies and was about to enter his father's antique business, had even tried to entice Gershom away from the hazards of the open road by offering him a job. But Gershom declared that he enjoyed the challenge of travel; besides, it was the only work he really knew, learned almost at his father's knee. He found no pleasure in admiring the patina of fine silver or puttering around with old coins.

On Gershom's next trip to Kreslavka, just months before the terrible pogrom there, he was a guest at the *bris milah* of Itzik's firstborn son. He later heard that Itzik had left for Germany.

It was only by chance that their paths had crossed again, years later, after Gershom had embarked on his career as a courier. Gershom had been given a message to deliver to Baron Isaac Rothenberg, a German Jewish nobleman who lived in England and summered in Russia.

He recalled that moment with relish. Entering the Baron's fine house, he was greeted by a footman who took his name, scrutinizing the peddler with disdain. Moments later, the seemingly chastened butler returned to invite him into the Baron's study. Amid the exquisite furnishings and the glitter of silver and crystal, the Baron sat behind a massive desk of gleaming, polished mahogany. When Gershom saw his smiling face, his knees turned to rubber. "Itzik?"

The Baron rose. "Gershom!"

The two fell into each other's arms.

"Gershom, you haven't changed at all," the Baron said with a warm chuckle.

"But you," Gershom stammered, his astonishment unhidden, "you are Baron Isaac Anshel Rothenberg? I can hardly believe it."

"Yes, my dear friend, the hand of God has taken me a long way from Kreslavka. And here I am," he said with an ironic smile, "the wealthy and envied Baron."

Though the years had separated them, their early bond of friendship had remained firm. And now it was time to test it.

A light drizzle accompanied him on most of his trip to Sumilino, where the Baron summered with his wife, Lady Clara, and their two lovely daughters, Sarah and Rebecca. Outside of a small circle of close friends, few knew why the Baron made anti-Semitic Russia his summer residence. Most could not fathom why the Baron would want to refresh his spirit in the land of Czar Nicholas the First rather than remain snug and secure in the family's Buckinghamshire estate or in one of the many renowned European resorts.

Yet duty beckoned the Baron to Russia. Using his wealth and influence, he continually tried to soften the Czar's draconian decrees against his Jewish subjects. In particular, he fought for the repeal of the brutal Cantonist Laws, under which Jewish children were conscripted into the army and then confined in "educational" camps called cantons. Everyone knew that this alleged preparation for army life was in fact a none-too-veiled attempt to convert the children to Christianity. And even if they miraculously survived the brutal regime as Jews, their subsequent twenty-five years in the Russian army would inevitably place an almost insurmountable barrier between the conscripts and their heritage.

Gershom was one of the few who knew of the Baron's special concern for these children. And he knew to what lengths his friend had gone to save them. Now he was certain that he could count on his generosity.

By the time he reached the Baron's home he was soaked to the bone, as well as exhausted and disheveled from his long, overnight journey. He presented his card to the Baron's footman and waited in the spacious foyer, trying not to sully the pink marble floors with his dripping clothing. He was admiring the shelves filled with curious jade and Chinese porcelain, when Lady Clara greeted him.

"On behalf of my husband and myself, welcome to our home, my dear Reb Gershom. The Baron will be with you shortly," she added in her usual gracious manner. "In the meantime, I will see to it that you are refreshed." She turned to the butler hovering solicitously in the background. "Cyril, please see to it that our friend Mr. Lader is made comfortable."

Gershom Lader thanked Lady Clara for her hospitality and followed the butler to a guest chamber. Over the years he had come to admire Lady Clara, a tall, strikingly handsome woman, the daughter of an Austrian banker, who was known for her great acts of charity and whose outstanding work among the poor had earned her the devotion of all who knew her.

Changing into dry clothing, Gershom awaited his old friend in the magnificent drawing room. It was already mid-morning, and he could see the sun shining on the verdant gardens through the large French windows. The garden was abloom with a profusion of flowers, and the lawns led to a private lake where two graceful swans glided regally on the silvery surface. Enveloped in this tranquil setting, Gershom was drinking in the beauty of the view when the Baron entered. The men rushed toward one another in an embrace of deep friendship.

"It has been far too long since we've seen each other," the Baron thundered, his arm flung across his friend's broad shoulder.

Gershom laughed, observing Itzik as if for the first time. No matter how many times he saw his friend, he was always astounded by Itzik's metamorphosis from a simple merchant into an elegant gentleman, though not, he was happy to note, into a dandy. The philanthropist's tastes remained on the side of genteel conservatism, and he looked impressive in his black waistcoat and white, carefully tied cravat. A high, velvet yarmulke partially covered his graying hair, and although he had become a bit portly, his face and eyes remained animated and one could still see the boy beneath the surface.

"My dear Itzik, you haven't aged a day. The good life seems to suit you," Gershom chuckled goodnaturedly.

"Prosperity may agree with me, but Gershom," he replied gravely, "I hope it is not poverty that makes you look so careworn. I pray that all is well with you and your lovely family."

"*Baruch Hashem*, they're well. It's just that at my age constant travel take its toll."

"So how long will you continue this dangerous work of yours? I worry about you, my friend. It's time to retire. Spend more time with your family, enjoy some peace of mind. There's still money in old coins, you know."

Gershom rose and walked over to the gilded fireplace. He lifted an andiron and examined it absently before replacing it. With his back to his friend, he began to discuss the purpose of his visit.

"I always feel guilty when I come to you with a plea for some worthy cause or other, Itzik, but you are the only one who can help."

The Baron joined his guest at the hearth. "Are you in financial difficulty, Gershom? I beg you, say no more. Whatever you need, consider it done," he said, grasping Gershom's shoulder.

Gershom shook his head. "You are a loyal and devoted friend, but thank God I have no need for help. It is not for my sake that I come all this way, but for the sake of two Jewish boys who have been captured by the Samoilov gang and are being held for an exorbitant ransom. Samoilov himself came to the home of Rabbi Yecheskel Marinberg of Ulla with his outrageous demand. And Rabbi Yecheskel, a fine human being, was certain that Samoilov meant every word of his threat to kill the boys unless he got his money. The Jews in Ulla have managed to raise two hundred rubles but the monster has demanded five hundred, an amount far beyond the means of the townspeople."

Gershom saw the Baron's lips twist into a grimace of pain; a veil seemed to fall over his eyes. The plight of two young boys trapped in the hands of a vicious anti-Semite had surely kindled memories that Itzik usually kept dormant. Gershom had feared, nay, expected this reaction. It was not to be helped; only the Baron could save the unfortunates!

Gershom glanced swiftly at the Baron, recalling the tragedy that had befallen Itzik just fourteen years earlier.

Thinking back on those nightmarish days, he thanked God for the miracle He had wrought, a miracle that had enabled his friend to rebuild his life from the ashes.

He was brought back from his reverie when Baron Rothenberg left his side and opened a strongbox standing near his desk. He took out a packet of rubles and handed them to a startled Gershom.

"Tell the good people of Ulla to keep their hard-earned money. Here is the five hundred rubles ransom. Just thinking about the boys' suffering at the hands of Samoilov grieves me and causes me more pain than anyone can imagine."

His eyes misted and he turned abruptly from Gershom. The peddler cleared his throat, fighting his own emotions. Nothing more was said between the men, except for the farewell pleasantries and the promise extracted from Gershom to bring his wife and children to Sumilino next summer.

With little time to spare, Gershom Lader raced back to Ulla, making but one stop on the way.

The Jews of Ulla waited nervously for the peddler to dismount and share his news with them. His smile was enough to reassure them that his mission had met with success. And when they discovered the full extent of the benefactor's generosity, they rejoiced.

The next day, at the appointed time, the Jews gathered in the town square. As Samoilov and his gang swaggered confidently into the village, a nervous hush fell over its inhabitants. The pale, bruised boys were untied and Rabbi Marinberg addressed them in Yiddish:

"*Ir zeinin Yiddishe kinder?*"

Reuven wiped away a tear. "Yes, we're Jewish children," he answered in a shaking voice.

The rabbi embraced them both and signaled to Reb Hershel to hand the rubles over to Samoilov, who counted the money greedily.

As the gang raced off, Gershom Lader smiled cryptically. The good Jews of Ulla had no way of knowing that Samoilov and his gang were in for a bitter surprise. For on his way back from the Baron's, Gershom had paid a secret visit to Sergeant Ivan Leonovich Donets, the head of the local constabulary. The sergeant had long been the recipient of generous gifts from Gershom in return for vital information about Jews. Over the years the two men had formed a cordial relationship. This time Gershom came to the sergeant with an ingenious scheme.

"So, my good friend," the sergeant had chortled warmly at the sight of his munificent Jewish friend, "what brings you to our fair community?"

"Tell me, Ivan Leonovich, what would you say if I could deliver Samoilov and his gang into your hands?"

"What would I say?" he grinned over his thick brush mustache. "You know that I would give my eyeteeth for that bunch of highwaymen. They have plagued these roads for years, and somehow they continue to elude us. Capturing that band of outlaws would surely earn me a promotion."

Sergeant Donets had literally jumped to his feet when Gershom Lader outlined his plan.

"Well done, my friend!" he cried, slapping Gershom

on the back. "We'll do our part, have no fear."

Gershom rose and shook the officer's hand.

"Remember, nothing should be done to endanger the two boys, is that clear?"

"Absolutely."

To assure the capture of the bandits, Gershom had also suggested that the police keep half the ransom money, if it was recovered. Ivan Leonovich agreed heartily.

Not long after the boys' rescue, Gershom received the happy news that Samoilov and his gang had been apprehended just outside Ulla. Two hundred and fifty rubles of the ransom was promptly dispatched to Baron Rothenberg with a note of explanation.

Yet the Baron quickly sent Gershom a note of his own:

My trusted and devoted friend,

I read your letter with joy. Lady Clara and I laughed heartily at your description of your transaction with the police. You never fail to amaze me with your exploits. May Hashem give you the strength and years to continue doing mitzvos. Now I beg you, please take the enclosed two hundred and fifty rubles and give it to tzedakah. I know I can trust you to find a worthy cause.

Your faithful friend,
Itzik

Gershom chuckled. Just like Itzik, he thought. He looked down at the money and made his decision. On his return to Ulla, he turned over the money to an astonished Rabbi Marinberg. “I have no doubt that you will find a proper charity, my dear rabbi,” he said.

Chapter 9

ON THE SHABBOS following the boys' rescue, the entire Jewish community gathered in Ulla's fine synagogue to hear them *bench gomel.* Their sojourn in Ulla, amid the kindness and generosity of the town's Jews, was the balm Reuven and Archik needed to mend their tortured bodies. As they prepared to continue their journey, Rabbi Marinberg and his rebbetzin pleaded with the lads to extend their stay, pointing out that a week and a half was hardly enough time to recuperate from their ordeal.

"Stay with us for just another month," the rabbi appealed.

"We are grateful to you and to all the people of this wonderful community, Rabbi," Archik said, "but we hope to reach Lithuania before winter sets in and travel becomes impossible."

The rabbi rubbed his cheek, his eyes mirroring his thoughts. "We all know your fears. It is no secret that the army is offering a handsome ransom for you two," he said with a frown. "But I can assure you that you are quite safe in Ulla. Ours is an influential *kehillah*, and no harm will come to you as long as you remain here."

Reuven sent his friend a searching glance, hoping that he might consider the rabbi's invitation, but Archik shook his head.

"Please forgive us, Rabbi, but I must reach my aunt and uncle in Kovno as quickly as possible. It is a very personal quest, I'm afraid," Archik said cryptically. He paused for a moment. "We are forever indebted to you and your community. Without your generosity, and your friend's intervention, we would not be alive today."

"And without God's help, none of our efforts would have succeeded," Rabbi Marinberg observed.

The boys left Ulla with heavy hearts. As he bid them farewell, Rabbi Marinberg embraced them both and handed them their tefillin and *siddurim*, which he'd insisted the bandits return.

"I only wish I could do more for you children," Rabbi Marinberg remarked in parting. "You are both so young, yet you have suffered so much. Through all your trials, I know that your faith in Hashem has never wavered." He then placed his hands on their heads and blessed them: "May the Lord bless you and guard you...."

At dawn they pulled away from Ulla. The August sun filtered through a sultry haze, and a warm breeze barely stirred the air as they slowly drifted along the river's calm surface. The boys were grateful for the quiet. They both needed to reflect on the events of the past few weeks. In the silence of dawn they found new clarity. They had come face to face with the fragility of life, and they knew without a doubt that their rescue was nothing short of a miracle, an act of Divine *chesed*. In the midst of pain and darkness, they had felt the presence of *HaKadosh Baruch Hu*. The *Ribono shel olam* Himself had snatched them from the very jaws of the lion. Now, seated on the slow-moving raft, they closed their eyes and swayed to and fro, davening with the <<MI%-4>>kavanah of those who have suffered and escaped death.

There were no tasks to do. The current was taking the raft down the middle of the river. As the morning grew warmer, Reuven nodded off to sleep. Archik squatted by the raft's edge, still thinking about all that had happened to them. He had planned the escape from the cantonist hell, knowing full well that few such schemes succeed and recapture meant torture and certain death. He had not only placed his own life in jeopardy, but his friend's as well. Deep in his heart, he knew he had convinced Reuven to share the risks of flight because he did not want to face danger alone.

If the agony of the past weeks had taught him anything, it was that Reuven was a loyal and devoted friend. The more he thought about his own behavior, the more he regretted it. With all his chutzpah, in the end it was Reuven who had shown true courage; it was Reuven who never wavered in his faith; it was Reuven who overcame the evil of his tormentors with his steadfast refusal to submit to them. His own cleverness was nothing compared to his friend's strength. Reuven's faith had touched him so deeply that he resolved to do *teshuvah*. He would begin by opening his heart to his friend.

A high, hot sun was beating down on the river when Archik leaned over and placed his hand on his dozing friend's shoulder. Reuven stirred, groaning, his nap interrupted. Archik shook him gently, and Reuven forced open his heavy-lidded eyes.

"Reuven, I need to speak to you," Archik said with unexpected urgency.

The uncharacteristic desperation in Archik's voice forced Reuven awake.

"Is something wrong, Archik?"

"No, nothing is wrong," he said softly. "In fact, everything is right."

"What are you talking about?"

Tears spilled down Archik's cheeks. Reuven gaped at his friend in open-mouthed astonishment, as Archik mopped the tears with the back of his sleeve, making no apology for his sudden show of emotion.

"Reuven," he began, "you know I am not much good at being humble, so please be patient with me…. I will never forget how I first swaggered up to you in camp, acting like a veteran of the wars, yet you greeted me as an equal. You showed me kindness and ignored my arrogance. I don't know how you put up with me," he chuckled. "I guess this encounter with Samoilov has forced me to do some soul-searching, and I realize that I've been a miserable ingrate. I can only ask you to forgive me. I," he hesitated, "I just want to say that I've learned a lot from you, and I value your friendship."

Reuven tried to interrupt, but Archik ignored him and continued.

"Since we ran away from the army, you have shared everything with me—your life, your hopes, your dreams. But I...I've kept my feelings under lock and key. I mocked you when all you wanted to know was our destination. I can never repay your loyalty, but at least I can be a sincere friend. You have always been open and honest with me. Now it is my turn."

Archik's voice grew low and his face became somber as he began his long overdue narrative.

Penina Gottlieb wiped her hands on her apron, her brow furrowed with growing concern as her husband Avrum unfolded the letter. They both gasped when the rubles fell to the table. With the special care of someone unaccustomed to receiving letters, he placed the envelope on the table next to them.

Avrum Gottlieb, the milkman of Kozin, an unpretentious *shtetl* near Kiev, was a man in his mid-thirties, powerfully built, with a generous brown beard and eyebrows so bushy that they appeared to shadow his deep-set brown eyes. The father of four daughters, the youngest now age eight, he somehow managed to keep his family decently clothed and fed.

At last he adjusted his glasses and held the letter close to his nose.

"It's from Uncle Misha," he said, not glancing up.

"*Guttenyu*, not bad news?"

Avrum shrugged and then began reading out loud.

My very dear niece and nephew,

It has been far too long since we have written to one another and we pray that all is well with you and your lovely family. We, baruch Hashem, are all in good health. Our sons Baruch and Shmulik are in the yeshivah and Mendel is, thank God, happily married and the father of two sons and three daughters. We have much nachas from all of them.

Now the reason for this letter: Fanya and I would like you and your family to visit us over the summer. Naturally, we do not wish for you to pay for the long and costly journey, so please do not be offended by our enclosing money. There is a very good and happy reason for our desire to have you spend the summer with us, a reason that will become clear once you are here. Fanya and I will not take "no" for an answer, so we expect you with us the first week of Sivan.

With great affection,
Uncle Misha and Tante Fanya

"So, Avrum, what do you make of this invitation?"

Avrum Gottlieb was generally a man of few words. True to his nature, he stared down at the letter resting on the table and, rubbing his beard with a large, callused hand, muttered, "We'll find out soon enough, Penina."

But Penina would not be put off. "But if you ask me, Fanya and Misha have a *shidduch* for our Sheindel," she mused, her eyes twinkling.

"There's no use guessing. If it's a *shidduch* I don't think they would be so secretive. Besides, Sheindeleh is only fifteen."

"*Only* fifteen? You forget already that I was `only' fifteen when our *t'nayim* were signed. Fifteen is not too young, Avrum," she said with a glint in her eye. "You men don't realize how much time these things can take. One doesn't rush into a marriage after one meeting. There's *mechetunimshaft*, *yichus*, a dowry, and then *t'nayim*. To you, it's one, two, three. But we women know better," she chuckled, waving her finger at him.

Avrum smiled and ventured a sigh and a shrug. "So if it's a *shidduch*, it will be a *shidduch*. But I think my uncle has something else in mind."

"What else can he have in mind, I ask you? To you everything has to be complicated. I tell you it's a *shidduch*. If not a *shidduch*, why does the letter insist we bring the girls with us?"

"So what else should my uncle propose, that we leave four daughters behind and go away on vacation?"

So with great anticipation and just a trifle of trepidation, Avrum and Penina Gottlieb and their four girls undertook the long journey to Lithuania. When at last they arrived, the reunion was emotional, but the circumstances surrounding it remained shrouded in mystery. Only after they were rested, refreshed, and seated around the table in the Ehrlichmans' dining room did the conversation turn to the purpose of the visit. It began, oddly enough, with the beckoning cry of a hungry baby.

"Oy," Penina exclaimed with delight, "you didn't tell us that Mendeleh's baby girl was here. Where is the darling?"

Fanya rose without a word. Minutes later she returned to the dining room holding a bawling five-month-old in her arms.

Penina Gottlieb ogled the infant for a second. "I thought Mendeleh's baby was older. This one is a *pitzeleh*."

Fanya did not reply. Instead, she placed the crying baby in a cradle and set it beside her. When the infant continued yowling, Fanya leaned over, clucking and crooning to the hungry child.

"Be a good *yingeleh* and I will bring you something to eat in a minute." With those words, she left the room to prepare the child's food.

All eyes now rested on their host, but all they received in return was Misha Ehrlichman's cryptic smile.

"*Nu shoin*," Avrum Gottlieb grumbled.

"Let us be patient and wait for Tante Fanya to return. Then I will share my story with you."

When at last Fanya appeared with the child's meal, Misha Ehrlichman began.

"Several months ago, I received an urgent appeal to come to Riga. My great-aunt Leah was very ill. Her only son, Yossele, had long since left for America, and there was no one to take care of her. Of course, I went, but by the time I arrived I could only do the *chesed shel emes* for her. I arranged the *levayah* and *Kaddish*, and prepared to journey home.

"I was approaching the town of Sloka when I found myself in the midst of a gypsy encampment. The gypsies did not look like a pleasant bunch, and I half-expected to be robbed, or at best to be pressed into buying some silly trinkets. I began feeling around in my pocket for a few coins when a dark, elderly man with a pock-marked face drew near. Everything about him was menacing. I admit, I was nervous. Who can know what is in a gypsy's head?

"The man motioned for me to dismount. I was certain he wanted to steal my horse, but I was surrounded and had no choice. He indicated that I was to follow him toward a wagon at the far side of the encampment. I tried not to show my terror when I saw over a dozen men with stubbly chins, long sideburns, and heavy mustaches eyeing me. Their looks weren't friendly. As I approached what I assumed to be the man's dilapidated wagon, I observed an elderly woman wiping a child's runny nose.

"The gypsy turned to the woman and said something to her in their Romany language. Without a word, she rushed off and returned carrying something wrapped in filthy rags. She handed the bundle to the gypsy. He removed the dirty wrappings and I found myself staring at a circumcised infant. I could not hide my astonishment. Surely the child had been stolen. As if reading my thoughts, the gypsy said that he had found the baby in the forest several weeks earlier. Then he asked what I expected: 'You want to buy baby?'

"I asked him to tell me exactly where he found the infant and under what circumstances.

" '*We always make camp near Kreslavka. When* we come to town to get permit to set up camp, we find nothing but death. I see there was pogrom and many innocent people murdered. I say to my people, "We make no encampment here." Where there is evil, gypsies not stay. We not want curse of evil eye,' he said, making some kind of sign with his left hand.

" 'We are packing to leave when my woman hears something like bleating of sheep or goat. I say to her, "go get animal," and she goes to look for it. Instead she returns with starving infant boy. Says she found in basket under tree.'

"The gypsy turned toward a young woman suckling her child and said, 'She the one who save the Jewbaby.'

"I asked the gypsy how he knew the child was a Jew. The man laughed.

" '*You think I not know Jewish boy child?' he said, still laughing. Then he drew a crumpled piece of paper from his pocket and handed it to me.*

"Written in a fine Yiddish, but in a terrific hurry, were the words '*Hut rachmoines of mein kint, a Yiddishe kint, Aharon Leib ben Yitzchak, un der Ribono shel olam vet eich betzullen*'—'Have mercy on a Jewish child and the Almighty will reward you.' I can tell you now that it was difficult to hide my feelings. But I had to negotiate with this man for the baby and it was best that I not tip my hand.

" 'How much?' I asked, pretending indifference.

" 'One hundred rubles,' he stated flatly, eyeing me shrewdly.

" 'Too much,' I replied. 'Remember, if the police find out that you have a Jewish child, they'll think you kidnapped him. I don't have to remind you what the punishment for kidnapping is. I'll give you fifteen rubles. Take it or leave it.'

"As the gypsy considered my offer, I prayed that he would not call my bluff.

" 'Twenty and you take baby.' "

Misha smiled in the retelling. "The truth was that I only had twenty rubles with me. I figured if I offered fifteen, we could compromise on twenty. And I won my wager."

Penina wiped a tear from her cheek and Avrum swallowed hard. A long silence filled the room.

"I took the child to Kreslavka in the hope of finding his parents. All I found was chaos and heartbreak. No one knew of a baby hidden in the forest. Still I persisted. I went in search of the town's rabbi, only to learn," he continued with a groan, "that he and his entire family had been massacred. I went from household to household, from one tragedy to another, until I could no longer bear the pain. Alas," he said, throwing his hands in the air, "there was no one to claim the infant.

"I had no choice but to bring the child home. My Fanya, angel that she is, soon found a wet nurse for him, and since then he has thrived. We call the little fellow Archikel: Aharon Leib seems too grown up for him right now," he said with a smile.

"After a month we both realized that even with all the goodwill in the world, neither of us have the *koach* at our age to bring up a child. Whether I like to admit it or not, we are no longer spring chickens," he chuckled. "It was Fanya who thought of you, young people who could give a little boy a loving family. Our son Mendel already has a houseful, *k'nainahora*, and he agrees that you are the ideal parents for this little boy. He will bring you *mazel*, you'll see." And then, Misha added with a wink, "A son after four daughters, heh?"

A look of compassion shadowed Reuven's face as he listened to his friend. His brows knitted together, he bent over to touch Archik's shoulder lightly. "And then what happened?"

After a long silence, Archik replied. "Until my twelfth birthday, I thought that Avrum and Penina Gottlieb were my real parents, although I suspected that something was not quite right. The bullies in *cheder* would tease me and call me names, and they bloodied my nose more than once when I fought back. But my family kept their secret, assuring me that the insults were based on foolish gossip. I wanted so much to believe them that I willed myself to ignore what I heard. Several months before I was bar mitzvah, however, my father took me aside and told me the truth. For days I would not speak. I was furious. I felt betrayed and deceived. My mother did her best to explain, to reassure me that they loved me as their very own. I finally accepted my lot, but even then I began dreaming that one day I would return to Kreslavka to find my family. It was as if a magnet inside of me drew me there. Then one night, all my dreams were shattered: A group of men I had never seen before came to my father's house. They told him that the village had failed to produce enough conscripts and I was being taken in order to fill the quota. I can still hear my mother's wails and my father's protests...."

Reuven drew a deep breath. "So why aren't we heading for Kreslavka?"

"I've had a lot of time to think, and I realized it would be wiser to visit my aunt and uncle in Lithuania. I need to hear exactly what happened from Uncle Misha's lips. There are too many empty spaces, too many unanswered questions. Only then can I return to Kreslavka."

"I will be at your side as long as you want me to be," Reuven said hoarsely.

"Reuven," Archik muttered, "I have no right to ask you to give up your own dream for me any longer. I admit I'd like you to come, but you have your own life to lead. Whenever you want to leave, I will understand."

"Friends stay together, Archik," Reuven said quietly.

Chapter 10

THE SUN BLAZED hot as ever during the day, but the evening chill brought with it a portent of autumn. Slowly the raft, now weatherbeaten and moldy, drifted toward Lithuania, still many dangerous miles away.

One Thursday evening the boys came to the village of Disna. They hid the raft and stopped to daven *maariv* before exploring the village sleeping peacefully in the moonlight. The air was musky. As they strolled past tangles of cottages along jumbled lanes, the boys exchanged delighted glances: there were *mezuzos* attached to many doorposts!

They returned to the riverbank to await the dawn, burrowing their heads under their blankets and dreaming delicious dreams of spending Shabbos in the company of fellow Jews. Once again they would daven with a *minyan* and enjoy a festive Shabbos meal in a warm Jewish home.

They awoke early, washed, davened *shacharis*, and with growing anticipation, readied to set out for the village. The good rebbetzin of Ulla had wisely given them Jewish garb to wear when it was safe to do so. But she had wagged her finger at them as she handed them the neat bundles. "There are evil men in this world, my children," she said. "The *khappers* in our midst are ready to spill Jewish blood! The rabbi tells me that the army is still looking for you, so be very, very cautious."

With these words still ringing in his ears, Archik looked at his friend. "What do you think, Reuven? Should we risk it?"

Reuven clasped his hands between his spread knees, a tentative smile surfacing. "It's been such a long time since we've enjoyed a real Shabbos. I say we take a chance."

Archik grinned broadly, crinkles emerging at the corners of his eyes. "Let's change clothes."

Dressed as Jews, they jauntily headed for the village. The peace of the night had given way to great commotion, and they sensed that something special was taking place. This was more than the usual bustle of housewives making last-minute Shabbos preparations and children rushing to and fro to help with the million and one chores demanded of them.

The boys glanced at one another with heightened curiosity. They made their way down from the knoll, trying to avoid the brambles and thorny bushes that edged the narrow path leading to the village. The last thing they wanted to do was tear their shiny new clothing. So engrossed were they in sidestepping the sharp-toothed foliage that they almost walked into a young boy carrying two buckets of water over his shoulders.

The gray-faced nine-year-old hardly spared them a glance before shifting the weight on his thin frame and plodded on.

"Wait up a second, we'd like to talk to you!" Archik cried to his retreating back.

The lad turned his head their way for a split second. "I can't stop. My momma's waiting for me and I gotta get the water home or she'll give me a thrashing."

"We'll help you with the buckets of water," Reuven called out, "if you'll just answer a couple of questions."

The boy stopped in his tracks. "You will?"

Reuven smiled. "It's as good as done," he said as he shouldered one bucket and Archik relieved the child of the other.

"So now can we ask you a question?"

The boy smiled sheepishly, revealing uneven teeth. "What kinda question?" he replied, giggling.

"Well, for one thing," Reuven probed, "why all the excitement in your *shtetl*?"

The boy scratched his ear, all the while prodding Reuven and Archik to make haste. "You mean you don't know about the smallpox epidemic?"

"No," Archik admitted, more perplexed than ever. "What does a smallpox epidemic have to do with so much hustle and bustle? It looks more like preparations for a wedding!"

"You mean you haven't heard how *HaKadosh Baruch*

Hu spared our village and not even one person came down with the pox?"

Archik and Reuven exchanged glances.

"Hey, what's your name?" Archik asked the excited child.

"Rafael, but everyone calls me Fulleh."

"So, Fulleh, what kind of festivities are planned for this special Shabbos?" Reuven eagerly inquired.

"You sure you aren't making *choizek* of me?"

"No, we're not making fun of you, believe us. We come from far away and we know nothing of what is happening in your village. We didn't even know there was a smallpox epidemic."

The child eyed them with a trace of skepticism. "Well," he drawled, "if you promise you're not teasing me...."

"Our word of honor," Reuven replied earnestly.

"Well, in that case," he said somewhat petulantly, "I can tell you that a new *sefer Torah* is being written and today the *sofer* is giving every child in the village the chance to write a letter in it before it is placed in the *aron kodesh*!"

The boys almost dropped their burdens as they stared at Rafael.

"Tell us, Fulleh, where does your rabbi live?"

The lad pointed to a nearby cluster of cottages. "It's the white house with the green tiled roof. There's a garden in front," he said by way of clarification, "and it's just behind the shul."

"And your rabbi's name?" Reuven asked.

"Rabbi Sholom Alterman. And he's a *tzaddik*," he added with a touch of pride.

After delivering Rafael and his two pails of water to his home, Archik and Reuven wandered about the village, drinking in the excitement. Finally, they followed the surging crowd toward the modest, one-room synagogue.

Dressed in their Shabbos best, a joyous swell of men and boys fought for a foothold inside the shul, every father eager to see his son called up to help the *sofer* write a letter in the new *sefer Torah*. Reuven and Archik listened attentively as each child's name was called. The children scrambled over to the scribe, placed their pudgy hands over his, and traced a character with him. Reuven turned to his friend and confided, "I would give anything to write a letter."

Archik pushed him forward. "Go on, go ask the *gabbai*."

Reuven blushed. "I...I can't. I don't feel I have the right to ask for such an honor."

Archik shook his head in irritation, grabbed Reuven by the arm, and elbowed his way through the crowd. Before Reuven knew what was happening, they stood facing the *gabbai*.

A short man with a beak-like nose and bushy eyebrows that almost obscured his eyes, the *gabbai* glared at the boys. "What do you mean by pushing your way up front?" he growled.

After a moment's hesitation, Archik leaned toward the *gabbai* and whispered, "Please forgive us, but my friend and I have traveled a long and hard road, and the hand of the *Ribono shel olam* brought us here to spend Shabbos in your village. We are escaped conscripts."

The *gabbai*'s thick brows rose and fell in one swift motion. He gazed open-mouthed at the boys, but before he could utter a word, there was a commotion nearby. Rabbi Sholom Alterman, the venerable rav of the village, had risen to his feet.

The rabbi was bent with age, yet his face radiated wisdom. He approached Archik and placed both his frail hands on the boy's shoulders. "Although I did not hear the words you whispered to our *gabbai*, my heart has revealed them to me."

His voice was as reedlike and fragile as his body, yet Archik and Reuven were riveted in place by its hidden power.

"Are you the boys who were recently in Ulla?" he asked.

Reuven muttered a strangled, "We are."

The rabbi turned to the astounded *gabbai*. "These boys are each to write a letter in the *sefer Torah*, and I will give *tzedakah* on their behalf," he said softly. "They shall complete the *sefer* with their letters."

Unaware of who the lads were or why they were being given this special honor, the entire congregation exhaled in one loud gasp, for it was known far and wide that Rabbi Sholom's great piety gave him special insight.

The *gabbai* led Reuven and Archik to the *sofer*, an ascetic-looking man with a white beard. He beckoned to Reuven. For a brief moment, he held Reuven in his gaze.

The scribe took Reuven's trembling hand and placed it on his own, skillfully etching the letter *reish* of the word "Yisrael" on the parchment before him. Next he called Archik to his side. Overcome with emotion, Archik faltered as he positioned his own hand over the scribe's. The *sofer* looked up. "It's quite all right. The *aleph* you have written is clear." He then whispered something to Archik. It seemed to Reuven that his friend had written still another letter but he shook his head in disbelief. It must have been his imagination.

Both boys stammered their gratitude as they left the scribe's side, and a huge cheer of "*Mazel tov*!" shook the tiny building to its very rafters. To compound their excitement, Rabbi Alterman invited them to spend Shabbos in his home.

A few hours later the boys returned to the synagogue, where a hushed assemblage had once again gathered. The *gabbai* and the distinguished-looking head of the *kehillah*, Duvid Feuerstein, ascended the *bimah*. Drawing aside the deep blue, velvet *paroches*, they removed the *sifrei Torah* from the *aron kodesh*. Four members of the congregation then unfurled a beautifully embroidered maroon, velvet <<MI%-2>>chuppah. The scribe handed the new Torah, swathed in blue velvet with gold embroidery, and wearing an exquisite silver crown, to Rabbi Alterman, who held it tightly to his breast. Standing beneath the *chuppah*, the rabbi waited solemnly as the *gabbai* and Mr. Feuerstein approached with their two Torahs to welcome the new Torah to their synagogue. The entire congregation broke out in song. "*Sisu v'simchu, b'simchas Torah*!" they rang out. "Rejoice in the gladness of Torah!"

That night the rabbi and his rebbetzin joyously welcomed the boys. Seated at the rabbi's *tish*, Reuven and Archik enjoyed Shabbos as never before, licking their lips in relish as they sank their teeth into the rebbetzin's delicious gefilte fish, chopped onions with *gribenes* and eggs, tender boiled chicken, and sweet, brown bread kugel laced with raisins and chicken fat.

Rabbi Alterman sensed that the lads were hungry for *divrei Torah* as well, so after a lively round of *zemiros*, he spoke to them about the *parashah*, wisely addressing them on a level they could understand. "*Meineh teireh kinder*, my dear children," he began in a voice deep with feeling, "in *Parashas Va'eschanan*, which we read this Shabbos from our new *sefer Torah*, Moshe reminds the Jews that Hashem took them out of Egypt to be His nation. He calls Egypt a *kur habarzel*, a crucible.

"Do you boys know what a crucible is? The artisan places an impure piece of metal within it. Then he turns on heat: blasting heat, fiery heat, heat that is almost unbearable. And, when all is done, the artisan peers into his crucible at the result of his labors: not an impure metal, but gold, gleaming gold.

"Hashem sent the Jews to Egypt to work as slaves in order to cast out their impurities and make for Himself a nation, pure and great. Sometimes we must suffer; sometimes the heat seems unbearable. But it ends, in the crucible, with pure, glowing gold.

"Remember the *kur habarzel*, my children, as you go on your way."

After Shabbos, Reuven and Archik were the guests

of honor at the *melaveh malkah* in honor of the new *sefer Torah*. Already stuffed from the rebbetzin's wonderful Shabbos repast, the boys nevertheless could not resist the handsome carp heads, stuffed geese and ducks, and *tzimmes* set before them. "Reuven," Archik playfully nudged his friend, "if only we could come upon a new *sefer Torah* being written every week."

Chapter 11

THE GRAY SKY brought with it a fine, light drizzle. Reuven and Archik huddled together under their tarpaulin shelter, their teeth chattering with the sudden drop in temperature.

"Something wrong?" Reuven asked, eyeing his friend's unusually wistful expression.

Archik shrugged. "Maybe it's the change in weather."

"It does look like we're in for a storm. Think we'd better head for shore?"

"I don't know. Maybe we can ride this one out."

"You think so?" Reuven muttered, staring up uneasily at the darkening sky.

"If things get too rough, we can always paddle in."

Reuven observed his friend from out of the corner of his eye. After a moment of silence, he clapped his hand on Archik's shoulder.

"It's more than the weather that's bothering you, isn't it, Archik?"

Archik avoided Reuven's penetrating gaze. When he finally spoke, his voice was so low Reuven strained to hear.

"I don't know how to explain it. I think you understand my feelings better than I do." Archik paused, staring ahead. "Ever since we left Rabbi Sholom, I've had this peculiar feeling of emptiness, sense of loss, as if I've left part of myself behind in that little *shtetl.* I keep thinking about the rabbi, seeing him before me. I don't know how to put it exactly," he shook his head and rubbed his chin thoughtfully, "but I still feel his presence, his holiness.

"For some reason I keep thinking about something my father told me when I was a child, an incident I haven't thought of in years. I must have been about four or five at the time. He had just returned from a visit to an elderly aunt in a nearby town. Even at my age, I noticed that my father, who was usually exhausted, looked contented, almost radiant. He turned to me and then, to my unexpected delight, he gave me a packet of chocolates—an unheard of luxury in our home. He told my mother that he had had the *zechus* to meet his rebbe. He said he was a true *tzaddik.* I remember wondering what a *tzaddik* looked like, and where I could find one. I really didn't understand what he was talking about. But now I know what made my father so happy."

Reuven marveled at the change in his friend. Archik had not lost his sense of adventure, or his mischievousness, but he was certainly less brash and far more introspective. He had become a more sensitive person and a more caring friend. Suffering had undoubtedly deepened Archik's faith. This, then, was the *kur habarzel* that Rabbi Sholom had spoken of.

"I can't help thinking, Archik, that the hand of God brought us to Rabbi Sholom. What a *zechus* to write a letter in a *sefer Torah*. When I saw that we were writing the last word in the Torah, *Yisrael*, and that the *sofer* had allowed me the letter *reish*, for Reuven, my hand trembled."

"I had the same feeling, Reuven. The *aleph* and *lamed* that I wrote also are my initials." Archik reddened and turned away in embarrassment. "You know, Reuven, it was the *sofer* who told me to write the second letter, the *lamed*. The very last letter of the *sefer*."

"You never told me."

"I didn't want you to think that I was boasting."

"What I think," Reuven said with feeling, "is that you have been doubly blessed."

The drizzle cloaked the river in a deepening haze. The boys sat in silence, absorbed in thoughts of their past and present lives. A brisk gust of wind and the sound of paddling oars shook them from their reverie. Through the mist, they could make out the outline of a raft no more than twenty feet away.

Reuven gasped. "Could it be Yussel Poznansky, the boy we met in the cave?"

Archik peered through the fog. "For his sake, I hope it's not. By now he should be halfway to Odessa, not heading for Lithuania."

A voice called out in Russian. "Hey you! What'cha doin' out here?"

Both boys heaved a deep sigh. It was surely not Yussel, but rather a local peasant lad out fishing.

Sure enough, as they drew closer they saw a boy on a log raft holding a makeshift fishing line.

"Catch anything today?" Reuven called out cheerily, not wanting to rouse suspicions by ignoring him.

The lad proudly held up a straw basket filled with squirming fish. "The rain brings them in. Best time to go out and fish, my father says, and he's right."

Reuven and Archik exchanged looks. There was plenty of good kosher fish available in the river—carp, bass, and perch—and by fishing they could keep their bellies full without forever worrying about finding their next meal. Never mind that neither knew a thing about fishing, and that the whole business was messy and unappetizing.

"Hey, fella, what do they call you?" Archik shouted.

"Vasily. And you?"

"Nikolai, and my friend here is Yuri. We're from up north. Heard of Volchov?"

"Nah. So what are you guys doin' so far from home?"

"No food, no work."

"Yeah, things ain't so good here, too."

Reuven thought fast. If they were going to learn to fish, they'd need help.

"Vasily, be a good fellow and help us," he said. "We lost our fishing gear in the storm, and to tell the truth our rod wasn't all that great, anyhow."

"Yeah, we never once filled a basket like you did," Archik added, flattering the boy. "Can you show us how you made your rod?"

"Nothin' to it," the boy replied, delighted by all the attention. "All you need is a birch branch with good bait tied to the end of the catgut. Maybe you fellas didn't have good bait. Whad'ya use, worms?"

Archik nodded unsurely.

"Figured as much. Nothin' better than grasshoppers, or if you're lucky, a small frog. Even a grub ain't bad," he said with a broad grin that could not be hidden by the fog. The boy checked his basket once again, pulled in his trolling line, and motioned for Archik and Reuven to follow him to shore.

Their raft secure, they scrutinized their new companion. Vasily was no more than twelve or thirteen, a pleasant lad with round cheeks. Moreover, he was clearly eager to share his expertise with older boys. No sooner had they landed than Vasily went hunting about for two flexible branches. "Got any catgut left?"

Palms upward, Archik shrugged. "All washed away."

"I guess I can spare a couple of lines," Vasily responded good-naturedly. The youngster hunted about once again, returning with a handful of small frogs, which he handed to a squeamish Reuven.

"You're in luck: rain brings out the frogs by the hundreds. Got somethin' to put the bait in?"

Archik pulled out a wicker basket from their gear. He took the squirming load from his friend, who looked as green as the frogs themselves, and chucked them into the basket.

"I'll give you one of my hooks, and you can make another couple from shells or thorns. They work pretty good, too."

"Thanks a lot, Vasily," Archik said, clapping the boy on the back and handing him three kopeks. "We really appreciate all your help."

The boy took the money, his eyes wide with gratitude. "Hey, thanks, guys." He scratched his thatch of dank, mouse-colored hair, his face screwed up in thought. "You got a couple more kopeks between ya?"

Reuven shot Archik a nervous glance. "Why?"

"Listen, stay here for a couple minutes. I got somethin' hidden in the brambles over there. Maybe you guys wanna buy it?"

"Okay, let's see," Archik replied, not very eagerly.

The lad dashed off and within minutes returned with something wrapped in a beautifully embroidered shawl. He opened it with a flourish and revealed a magnificent *shofar*.

It took everything they had not to exhale a gasp of astonishment. "What's that?" Archik asked as casually as he could.

"A special kinda horn the Jews use in their church."

"How'd you get it?" Reuven inquired uneasily.

"I found it," he chuckled and winked.

"Where?" Reuven pressed.

"There're some Jews in a village about five miles down the river, in the direction of Volyncy. When no one was around, I just walked in and took it."

Reuven put the *shofar* to his lips, pretending to blow. Not a sound came forth.

"It doesn't seem to work," Reuven concluded, to Vasily's chagrin.

Archik took the treasure from Reuven and tried to look it over as if seeing a *shofar* for the first time. "Well, if it doesn't work, why should we want it?"

"Maybe you guys can sell it to someone," Vasily urged. "I'll give it to you for three kopeks."

Archik eyed Reuven. "What do you think?"

"I don't know. It doesn't work."

"All right, two kopeks."

"One kopek," Reuven offered, handing the lad the coin.

"Ahh, okay. I ain't got no use for a broken horn, anyway."

Waving to Vasily, the boys shoved off, happy to be on their way. There was no question about their next stop.

Reuven and Archik docked near Volyncy for the night. Dawn was no more than a shimmering promise when they began their trek. Their only source of light was a blood-red harvest moon, which crept stealthily through mountainous clouds. The summer rain had made the ground muddy and slippery. Sloshing their way along a narrow path riddled with puddles, they could only hope they were heading toward the village Vasily had spoken of.

They had trudged down the path for almost an hour when Reuven pointed to something in the distance.

"Do you see something out there?"

Archik peered through the thickening fog. His face brightened. "I think that's it. Come on, Reuven, let's make a run for it."

Their well-worn boots squishing in the mud, they raced toward the dim outline of buildings, managing to reach the slumbering village just as dawn's light broke through the mist.

The village was no more than a pathetic smattering of cottages and barns. Not even the rain could cleanse the ugly blotches of unrelenting poverty. Maneuvering through flooded lanes and down alleys gushing with streams of water, they listened to the barn animals greeting the new day.

"What do you think, Reuven?" Archik asked. "Should we try to find the rabbi's house?"

Archik paused, trying unsuccessfully to remove a pebble from his mud-stained boot. "I don't know, Reuven, I...."

He stopped short. Before him stood a wooden house, slightly larger and less weatherbeaten than the others. Even in the haze, the boys could make out the flag waving dismally in the sharp breeze. The eagle emblazoned upon it, sign of the Romanovs, seemed to glare at them, as if ready to seize them with greedy talons. It was clearly some sort of official building, which only meant one thing: Danger!

"Forget the rabbi," Archik said, an edge of panic in his voice. "Let's get out of here, Reuven."

Reuven shook his head. "Look, Archik, we're *shelichei mitzvah*, so what can happen to us? I say we find the shul and return the *shofar*."

Archik reluctantly agreed, and they walked on cautiously.

They examined every structure, anxious to find the synagogue before being observed. Despite Reuven's assurances, apprehension remained with them like an albatross around their necks. They had a sinking feeling that Kolchak was breathing down their necks; every shadow spelled disaster. Nor did they forget the *khappers*, the Jews hired by the desperate *kehillos* to kidnap children in order to meet the Czar's quotas.

Turning down a lane, they found themselves in a courtyard matted with weeds and foliage. The wooden building in its center seemed sturdier than most other houses in the village, and the coat of whitewash less yellow. Upon closer observation, they could see the outline of a menorah over the lintel.

The synagogue door was padlocked, so the boys circled the small structure in search of another entrance.

"Look up there," Reuven whispered, pointing to a window about ten feet from the ground. "Do you think we could get through?"

Archik looked up, wiping away the rain that splattered down his face and blurred his vision. "I think so."

"Good," Reuven said. "Hoist me up and leave the rest to me. You stay down here and stand guard."

The rusty window bolt resisted Reuven's efforts, but he persisted and eventually it gave way. Jiggling the creaking window open just enough to squeeze through, he jumped to the floor. With the carefully wrapped *shofar* held close to his breast, he stopped to catch his breath and examine the shadowy images of *shtenders* and long tables with *siddurim*. A feeling of longing swept over him.

Reuven looked down at his precious cargo. With Elul just days away, the Jews of this village would once again have their beautiful *shofar*. Again his eyes scanned the small synagogue. He was suddenly beset by a heart-wrenching thought: Would he and his friend live to hear the *shofar* once more? He pressed the ram's horn to his heart. He had never before given in to his doubts, but now, standing in the synagogue, he realized that fear of failure was always just beneath the surface.

He walked slowly toward the *aron kodesh*, opened its wooden doors, and drew back the worn, blue, velvet *paroches*. Two *sifrei Torah* rested within. Tears rimmed Reuven's lids as he bent over and kissed the Torah scrolls. He replaced the *shofar* lovingly and closed the doors and the *paroches*.

Were those footsteps? His heart almost stopped. Dawn had lifted the veil of night and the villagers would soon be heading to shul for *shacharis*. He heard Archik's loud whisper warning him that someone was approaching. He had to get out.

Yet Reuven remained frozen, his heart pounding.

Even as he heard the key turn and the door squeak open, he stood glued in place. A shaft of light pierced the gloom, missing him by inches. Reuven wrenched himself from his trance-like state, dashed toward the window, and lowered himself out of the synagogue seconds before the man entered.

Reuven and Archik sprinted toward the village's outskirts, avoiding the townspeople on their way to prayer. When they were well away from the village, the two collapsed, exhausted and indifferent to the muddy ground. A minute or two passed in silence. Then Archik gazed at his companion.

"Reuven," he sputtered, "you should see yourself now!"

Reuven returned Archik's laugh with a quivering grin. "You don't look all that great, either!"

Wiping the tears of laughter with his muddy hands, Archik pushed himself to his feet and pulled Reuven after him. Through bursts of strangled guffaws, he choked, "Let's get back to the raft and get cleaned up. Maybe you haven't noticed, but it's time to daven *shacharis*."

As the two mud-covered apparitions made their way towards the safety of the river, Reb Yonah, the cobbler of the tiny hamlet of Tuvin and the *shammas* of its shul, sadly approached the *aron kodesh*. Since the theft of their *shofar*, it was his melancholy duty to inspect the contents of the *aron* daily and make certain all was well.

The disappearance of the *shofar* had hit Reb Yonah particularly hard. Neither a scholar nor a man of means, serving as *shammas* was his way of serving God. And now, despite the rabbi's protestations to the contrary, Reb Yonah felt responsible for the loss. Rosh Hashanah was fast approaching—what would their impoverished village do this year?

With a heavy heart, he pulled open the velvet curtain and opened the wooden doors. He stared, shook himself, stared again. Could it be? Was this an illusion? Extending a leathery hand, he touched the *shofar* gently, as if it might disappear. It was intact and as beautiful as ever. His eyes closed as he pressed the *shofar* to his lips.

So the congregation found him that morning. The room grew hushed as the rabbi approached Reb Yonah and placed his hand on the man's bent shoulder.

"Rabbi, the *shofar*..." he said, his words choked with emotion.

The rabbi nodded. "Yes, Reb Yonah, our prayers have been answered."

Reb Yonah handed the *shofar* to the rabbi and wept unashamedly.

Chapter 12

A BRISK AUTUMN wind ignited the kindling and soon two good-sized, freshly caught fish were sizzling over the fire. Reuven edged closer to the flame, hugging himself against the evening chill. The tantalizing aroma made his mouth water, although he readily admitted to Archik that he found fishing a loathsome pursuit. The very sight of a hapless bass wiggling on his line made him queasy, and he was happy to leave the distasteful tasks of cleaning and preparing the fish to his unperturbed friend.

The weeks had flown by and the balmy days of summer had been supplanted by blustery autumn evenings. The cool winds sent shivers down their spines, and not just due to the cold. They were far more concerned that an early frost would make rafting to Lithuania an impossibility.

But for the moment at least, their thoughts were on

the delectable repast grilling on the spit, and on their gratitude to God for His bounty. As dusk crept across the sky, they davened *maariv* under a canopy of burnished red and gold leaves, swaying to and fro in heartfelt prayer. After their meal, the boys turned in for the night. With their bodies resting on a bed of crackling leaves, they inhaled the pungent autumn bouquet until sleep overtook them.

Sometime between midnight and dawn, Archik woke with a start. He lay quietly, listening. What was it that penetrated his deep sleep, he wondered? He could see nothing in the moonless night, but a sixth sense alerted him to danger. There was something out there, something sinister close by. Archik felt certain they were not alone. He touched his friend's arm lightly, but Reuven only groaned and turned away. In desperation, Archik leaned over and cupped his hand over Reuven's ear.

"Reuven, wake up. We've got company."

"What?"

"Shh," Archik whispered. "We may have to get away fast."

Now fully awake, Reuven held his breath and listened intently. Both boys could hear neighing horses. Their bonfire long since sputtered into cold ashes, they gathered their gear in the darkness. Crouching low to avoid the branches, they headed toward their hidden raft, hoping to paddle to safety. Suddenly, a deep, commanding voice shouted for them to halt.

"Do you think it's Kolchak?" Archik whispered.

"God forbid!"

"Whoever it is, we're in for it," Archik mumbled under his breath.

The shadowy figure of a man mounted on a large horse prodded them through the woods. They soon reached a knoll where, to their astonishment, they saw a dozen bonfires. In the murky light of the smoking blazes they finally made out their captor, a huge, mustachioed man in cossack uniform.

Cossacks! Every Jewish child had heard of these Ukrainian soldiers, members of one of the Czar's most elite—and brutal—military units. Throughout the Russian empire, the word "cossack" was synonymous with pogroms. And now they had fallen into the hands of an entire brigade of them!

"Who are you?" the soldier asked them gruffly.

Archik repeated his now well-rehearsed story.

The cossack pushed them closer to one of the fires and scrutinized them with a professional eye.

"Those are mighty fine jackets for poor boys to be wearing."

Reuven forced a grin. "We did some work on Count Kropotkin's estate and his servant paid us with the jackets."

The cossack eyed the boys more intently. "Did you meet the Count?"

"Yes, sir," Reuven replied.

"What's he look like?"

Reuven gave an accurate description of the handsome young Count.

The cossack greeted Reuven's response with a tight smile as he drew his hand along his luxuriant mustache. "That's him, all right. If the Count let you work for him, you must be honest, so you're free to stay here for the night. It's safer, believe me," he laughed.

The boys exchanged glances. "Thank you, sir," Archik replied, trying to sound grateful.

The cossack introduced himself as Sergeant Grisha Denisovich Zolochov and left them to bed down for the night as he returned to his watch.

"That's all we needed, a platoon of cossacks," Archik said with a groan.

"So what? Tomorrow, we'll just thank Zolochov for his hospitality and be off."

"From your mouth to God's ears," Archik sighed.

Despite his optimistic words, Reuven felt uneasy. When he finally fell asleep, he was disturbed by strange dreams. He saw his father before him. He ran to hug him but the image drifted away. From afar, he could hear his father warn, "Remember the Chmielnicki pogroms." His voice was deep with emotion, as if the massacres had taken place yesterday, and not two hundred years earlier. His father's wavering form reappeared before him. Again Reuven tried to embrace him, but again the image withdrew. "Beware the cossack murderers," his father intoned.

Reuven woke, his body soaked with perspiration. He struggled to still his pounding heart. The dream had been so vivid, so menacing. He watched the dawn glow pink over the horizon and listened to the sound of men stirring. He washed his hands and automatically reached for his tefillin; then he drew his hand back as if burned. On this brilliant autumn morning, he knew that he and his friend would not have the opportunity to put on tefillin or daven. He closed his eyes to erase his despair, and his father's words came to mind: "Beware the cossack murderers." He felt more certain than ever that his father had come to warn him of impending danger. They had to escape these devils, to somehow get away.

When the other cossacks rose, Sergeant Zolochov appeared at Reuven and Archik's side, eager to show off his find. He led them to Lieutenant Igor Ivanovich Kolguyov, a tall man with a deeply tanned, weathered face, a thick, rust-colored beard, and steel-gray eyes that seemed to pierce the boys as he spoke.

This time it was Reuven who took the initiative. "We wish to thank you for letting us make camp with you last night. But now we must be on our way. We have a long trip ahead," he said briskly. "We are heading for Lithuania, to Nikolai's relatives. They have a farm near Vilna and they may have work for us." He looked up at the sky before adding, "We hope to get there before the frost."

Sergeant Zolochov roared with laughter as the lieutenant placed both hands on Reuven's shoulders, his eyes twinkling.

"I like boys with spunk and imagination," he chuckled. "But there's no need to go off to Lithuania. We'll find work for you here. The fact is, we were looking for a couple of strapping lads to groom the horses. Who knows, if you prove yourselves loyal and capable, you might even join the cossacks. What better future for a young man, heh?"

Reuven felt his knees buckle as he returned the officer's smile. He searched for a way out, but his mind went blank. He was too stunned to speak.

Fortunately, Archik burst out, "That's wonderful, sir. But we are just ignorant peasants, certainly not worthy to be asked to join the Czar's valiant warriors."

The sergeant leered at the boys. "Are you turning down our offer to serve the Czar?"

"Heaven forbid," Archik exclaimed, his voice earnest. "We would be deeply honored. But who are we to be given such a privilege?"

"I like these lads," the lieutenant retorted. "Their modesty shows intelligence and becomes boys of their station." Turning toward them, he abandoned his former friendliness, and spoke in a tone that invited no further argument. "In the name of the holy Czar, I command you to join our ranks. If you follow orders, you will be well treated. If not, you will soon discover what we do to those who shirk their duties."

Archik and Reuven were well equipped to deal with the tight discipline in the cossack camp. They quickly learned to keep the horses nicely groomed and well fed, and gave the sergeant no reason to be anything but satisfied with their diligence.

Others were less fortunate, and the boys gritted their teeth at the sight of the punishment they received, which brought to mind their cantonist days. The lash was used on any cossack who dared to break the rules, and defiance was all too common within the platoon of rough, violent men, mostly Ukrainian peasants.

They had fallen into a pit of vipers, and day and night Reuven and Archik plotted escape. They had outwitted more diabolical oppressors, Archik reasoned, and there had to be a way out of this new bondage. But try as they would, no plan came to mind. The camp was too well guarded.

In desperation, Archik tried to insinuate himself into the ranks, hoping to charm the men into turning a blind eye to their escape. His blond good looks and sharp wit soon made him a favorite of Corporal Grigor Feodorovich Shevenchko, who was a bit older than the others and took a fatherly interest in him. One night on guard duty with the corporal, Archik tested the waters with a veiled reference to an escape plan. To his shock, he was angrily rebuffed by the loyal cossack, who spat at his feet as soon as the implication of Archik's words became clear.

The next morning, Archik was taught a painful lesson. It was only because of Sergeant Zolochov's intervention that the usual fifty lashes meted out for so serious an offense were reduced to a mere twenty. Archik was also put on bread and water rations for two days. Reuven could not hide his anguish as he smoothed healing salve on his friend's raw back and heard him whimper in agony.

It was clear that neither bribery nor friendship

offered escape. Nevertheless, despite his punishment, Archik was more determined than ever. There had to be a way out. He thanked God for his strong constitution, which enabled him to heal quickly. Before the week was out he was back on duty. The cossacks did not take kindly to deserters, but Archik's stoic endurance softened their hearts, and the carousing, hard-drinking men mostly left the lads in peace.

During the first weeks of their cossack slavery, the men moved steadily inland. With each passing day, the boys were taken farther from their raft and river escape route. At the end of the second week, Lieutenant Kolguyov gathered his platoon about him. The boys only caught a few of his words, but these alone were enough to chill their blood: "bayonets," "burn the village," "no prisoners."

That night they tried to piece together the phrases that had drifted their way.

"What if they are planning a pogrom?" Reuven despaired. "What should we do?"

Archik shook his head. "We don't really know whom they plan to attack."

"Who else but Jews?"

"According to my map and what I've heard in the camp, it seems there aren't too many Jews in these parts."

Reuven was not reassured. "We've found Jews in the least likely places, Archik. Who can say there aren't Jews here?"

Archik pulled at the thin, blond hairs that had budded on his chin. "We have no choice but to seek more details. I'll try to get something out of Pyotor. He's not much older than we are and he wants to be friendly."

"Be careful, Archik. Remember what happened the last time you tried to be buddies with one of them."

Archik waved away his friend's fears. "That was different. This is just going to be friendly conversation. Leave it to me."

The following day, Reuven noticed Archik saunter over to Pyotor and exchange some words with him. He couldn't read Archik's expression; all he could do was wait until nightfall, when they would have a chance to talk. But to his dismay, Archik was sent out on guard duty with Pyotor that night. Reuven slept fitfully. He had an uneasy feeling that the attack was planned for the next morning.

When the corporal shook Reuven awake at dawn, there was a lot of movement in the camp. Everyone seemed on alert. His eyes squinting against the hazy morning light, Reuven looked for Archik, but he was nowhere in sight.

"To your feet, Yuri Pavlovich," the corporal ordered. "The horses have to be saddled. We need every hand."

Reuven pulled himself to his feet, raced to the cistern to splash icy water on his face, and rushed off to his duties. In the lingering morning mist, he couldn't find Archik among the shadowy figures moving about the camp. He had just saddled up his third horse when he felt a hand on his shoulder. He whirled around but before he could utter a sound, Archik had placed a finger to his lips.

"We'll talk later. Just stay nearby," he whispered.

An icy wind had washed away the haze, and the rays of a weak autumn sun were casting eerie shadows over the plain. The cossacks rode slowly forward, each brandishing a naked saber and ready for battle. The two boys had been ordered to remain in the rear astride their two nags. Their task was to clear the field of the dead and wounded. Reuven closed his eyes and muttered a short prayer. In his uniform, sitting straight and tall in the saddle, Archik looked just like one of the dreaded cossacks. Reuven could not know that in his high fur hat, he looked no less terrifying.

The platoon was divided into three columns, with a line of officers in front. Clearly, a three-pronged assault was planned. But who and where was the enemy?

Reuven caught his friend's eye at last, his expression clearly questioning. Archik leaned over and explained, "They're attacking the village of Lopatovo."

"Lopatovo?"

"The cossacks got word that a group of peasant agitators there have worked up the villagers to demand the end of serfdom."

Archik brought his mount closer to his friend. "To make sure no one else gets any such revolutionary ideas, the Czar has ordered a massacre. That's what's planned for this village. Pyotor told me they are to show no mercy. Men, women, and children—no one is to survive."

Reuven swallowed hard. "How can they kill innocent people?"

"The same way they kill Jews. After all, what have we

ever done to the Czar? Have we Jews ever imperiled his rule? Have we ever been guilty of treason?"

"No," Reuven sighed. "And now all we can do is sit here and watch the slaughter. If only we could have warned them."

"I tried to think of a way, believe me, but I couldn't. But there is one chance in a thousand that they may have gotten wind of what is planned."

Reuven stared at his friend.

"Last night, on guard duty, when Pyotor left for a moment to check in with another sentry, I spotted a boy peering out at me from the brush. I motioned for him to come over. He was terrified, but curiosity got the better of him. I asked him where he came from and he pointed toward Lopatovo. I whispered that he was to go home and tell his father that the cossacks were attacking the next morning. The child looked at me as if I were crazy, then he ran off. Maybe he told his father. For their sakes, I hope so."

The villagers had just begun to stir. Several were harnessing their horses, others walked off to their fields; women and children, their aprons filled with corn, flung feed at the hungry chicks and ducks. Young boys carried mash to the pigpens or headed toward their barns, pitchforks in hand. It was a bucolic scene, a world away from blood and violence.

At the thought of what awaited them, Reuven felt the bile rise to his throat.

Suddenly the order was given and a shout went up. The cossacks spurred their battle-trained horses and charged down the hill. But then another shout rang through the air. Over fifty villagers grabbed stakes, scythes, knives, and pitchforks, mounted their farm horses, and surrounded the cossacks. With their oppressors stunned into inaction, the peasants slashed wildly into the platoon, hacking and bayoneting the cossacks to death.

Reuven and Archik raced back behind the lines, too overwhelmed to think about their next move. Away from the battle, they restrained their snorting horses long enough to take stock. "This may be our only chance!" Archik cried, catching his breath. Without a second thought, they spurred their horses to full gallop, hoping to be well on their way before the cossacks realized they were gone.

Unwittingly, however, they raced straight into the menacing arms of a group of triumphant peasants hungry for revenge. The boys' horses reared as the peasants prepared to charge their fresh quarry.

"We're prisoners, don't attack!" Archik shouted. A peasant, obviously the leader, held up his hand and the attack halted.

"Get off your horses," he ordered, his face hard and his eyes filled with distrust and hatred.

The boys dismounted. "Volya, check their gear."

A young man grabbed their knapsacks and dumped the contents to the ground. He glanced at the boys' meager possessions, kicking the tefillin to make sure they were not weapons. "They ain't got arms," he said.

Reuven licked his dry lips. The leader was shrewd,

and now they were in for it. Reuven tried to think how to explain away their tefillin and *siddurim*, but his mind went blank. He just hoped the peasants did not know what the tefillin were. Neither boy had any illusion about the virulent anti-Semitism of Russian peasants.

The leader eyed their belongings and scrutinized their faces. "Where are you boys from?"

Archik tried to swallow but his throat was too dry. "We're from Volchov, sir," he muttered. "We were rafting down the river on our way to Lithuania when the cossacks took us prisoners." Suddenly he got an idea. "Sir, I stood guard last night and warned a little boy of the attack!" he blurted out.

The peasant surveyed him thoughtfully. "You're a long way from the river," he said mildly. He turned unexpectedly to the others. "They're all right," he declared, motioning for the men to put down their weapons. He patted Archik on the shoulder. "We had a feeling they were coming, lad, but we weren't sure when. I sent out my boy as a scout and he returned with your message. Thanks to you, we got most of them. Now just race off and don't look back. They're an ugly lot and it's best you have nothing more to do with them."

"Yes, sir. And thanks for believing us," Archik said.

"You are not my enemy today. But next time keep your belongings better hidden," he warned cryptically. "You never know who'll find them, and others may not be indebted to you."

Chapter 13

MENACHEM MENDEL Rosen, a paunchy, middle-aged man with a rosy face and a disposition to match, had just finished a meal of hard-boiled eggs, thick slices of juicy onion, and black bread, washed down with a tumbler of fiery plum brandy. He recited *birkas hamazon* and closed his eyes to enjoy a siesta on a bed of fragrant pine needles.

A peddler of housewares and bolts of cloth, Menachem Mendel always kept a few steps ahead of one disaster or another. But today's calamity had left him unnerved; just thinking of it made him shudder.

For twelve long, hardworking years, his trusty horse Vanka had taken him over the many miles without complaint. And he, for his part, had been a good master, always remembering to give Vanka her oats and water, to cover her with a warm blanket, and to see that she was quartered in a clean, comfortable stall with plenty of hay and fodder.

But today, Vanka had gone lame, and with a heavy heart Menachem Mendel had sold her to a glue factory. Not only had he lost his faithful friend, he'd all but lost his livelihood. He was a peddler without a horse: about as useful as a tone-deaf fiddler.

Menachem Mendel was the first to admit that his chosen trade had never garnered him more than a poor living at best. Not that Perele, his devoted wife of nineteen years and the mother of eight noisy children, was not forbearing. He could only admire her talent for stretching a ruble as far as it could go and her dexterity with a needle and thread. He was never ashamed of the well-worn and well-mended clothing she produced, and no one, thank God, went hungry or barefoot in his home. But after buying a horse, even a cheap one, there would be little or no money left for his family. He groaned. He did not relish facing Perele with such catastrophic news. On the other hand, he reasoned, how could a peddler return home without a horse?

His head throbbed and his heart pounded. Sleep would simply not come. He stared down at his stubby, callused hands. What else was there for him to do in life? His father had been a peddler and so had his father's father. Yet one could not peddle without a horse and wagon—these were the essential tools of his trade. He pulled himself up with a groan and took another swig of brandy. The warming liquid began to soothe his tension and he once again curled up on his prickly bed and closed his eyes in the hope of a brief respite from his *tzurris*. But the idyl was shortlived.

Having long ago learned to disregard the forest clamor, it was not the din of the chirping birds that roused him from his reverie, but the unwelcome sound of human voices. Menachem Mendel struggled to his feet and edged his way stealthily toward the voices, his puckish faced screwed up as he strained to listen. A mild, non-violent man, Menachem Mendel nevertheless drew the revolver that he had acquired after one particularly nasty encounter with bandits had cost him his wares and almost his life.

The voices grew louder as he drew nearer to the river. He stooped low in an attempt to conceal himself in the tall bulrushes. Scanning the area, his eyes came to rest on two young *shkutzim* securing a raft to a tree. Though they appeared harmless enough, one could never be certain. He kept his eyes glued on them for a few moments and then, with a shrug, began stealing back to his own camp.

Suddenly, Menachem Mendel whirled about again, his heart beating rapidly. Had he heard the *shkutzim* speaking *mamma lushin*? No, he was not mistaken. As sure as day followed night, one of the lads had said in Yiddish, "First, let's gather twigs for a fire, and then we'll daven." He froze in place and held his breath lest he break the spell. He waited unobserved until the boys gathered their kindling. He saw them remove two *siddurim* from their knapsacks and begin swaying to and fro in prayer.

Menachem Mendel blinked several times, as if clearing the cobwebs from his eyes. His mind told him one thing and his eyes another. He scratched his chin under his scrawny beard and wondered: Why would pious Jewish boys raft down the river wearing the clothing of *goyisheh* peasants?

Curiosity finally overcame caution. When the boys finished praying, he brushed off the leaves and pine needles that clung to his jacket, tucked his revolver into the holster hidden under his jacket, and stepped out to make his presence known.

"A good day to you!" he boomed with a kindly smile.

The boys spun about. Though the man spoke Yiddish, experience had made them wary of all strangers. They hesitated before returning his greeting.

"You are *Yiddishe kinder*?" he inquired warmly.

"And who are you?" Archik countered.

"I am Menachem Mendel Rosen from Zhitomer, a peddler by profession," he replied. "The good Lord above has deprived me of my horse and I have had no choice but to leave my wagonful of goods in a barn in Druja, a town some ten miles east of here. I trudged all this way in the hope of finding a peasant willing to sell me one of his less worthy horses. Unfortunately, I am a man of modest means, and the only horses I can afford are older than I am, and one step away from the glue factory," he groaned. Then, forgetting his own troubles, he peered at the boys. "My lads, Purim is six months away. How is it you are already in costume?"

The boys exchanged uneasy glances. "We are looking for work. Our families are poor and we thought we could find jobs on a farm if we dressed as peasant boys," Reuven said.

Menachem Mendel pulled at his ear. "Maybe the *goyim* will believe such a story, but you can't fool me," he chuckled. "*Yiddishe kinder* don't wander in these parts looking to work for a peasant. You could earn the same few kopeks doing chores in your own villages," he said shrewdly. "So?"

"How do we know that you are an *erlicheh Yid* who's telling us the truth about yourself?" Archik declared, scrutinizing the man standing before him.

Menachem Mendel drew back as if slapped. He eyed the boys and then nodded his head as a clearer picture emerged. He was no fool, and he had taken stock of the situation. Now he understood what this *purimshpiel* was about. "I swear to you by all that is holy, I am not one of those vile *khappers*," he said, spitting the word out. "Have no fear, I wouldn't turn in a dead cat for their one hundred rubles."

Reuven sent Archik a searching look.

Menachem Mendel raised his hands, palms upward. "Reward posters have even reached these parts, I'm afraid. So I fully appreciate your caution. Only a fool would reveal himself in such times as these."

He extended his hand to the boys in a firm handshake. The man's open, honest face and reassuring words seemed to proclaim his sincerity, and Reuven and Archik at last introduced themselves, apologizing for their rude behavior. They immediately invited their guest to join them around the fire, and over mugs of tea they recounted their escapades.

Menachem Mendel exhaled a long breath as they concluded their story. "Well, my boys," he stated unequivocally, throwing his arms about their shoulders, "both of you could do with a bath and a good Shabbos meal."

"Are there Jews around here?" Reuven inquired hopefully.

"There's a small community in Druja. I know the rabbi, a *feiner Yid*, a good and kind man. I was heading back there myself," he said, "and you will join me. The rabbi and his rebbetzin are always happy to have company for Shabbos, and not too many Jews visit these parts." And then, with a broad wink, he added, "The rebbetzin is an outstanding cook and I can promise you roast goose this Shabbos."

Accompanied by Menachem Mendel, the boys trudged through the village without incident. At first the Jewish burghers stared at the lads, but then, they simply assumed that Menachem Mendel the peddler had engaged two *shkutzim* to help him cart his wares now that he was horseless. Reuven and Archik were grateful to avoid the usual interrogation.

The rabbi's house was unpretentious, like those of his neighbors: built of wood from the nearby forests, once sturdy and clean, now warped and beaten by the weather into a dull, dark brown. Only one house in the area boasted smooth walls and a brick fireplace, Menachem Mendel informed the boys: the home of Reb Shaya Sharman, *gabbai* of the shul and a man of means.

He hustled the lads into the rabbi's home, where they were met by the family servant, Katarina. At the sight of the visitors she called out, "Rebbetzin, Menachem Mendel has arrived," then fixed a curious eye on Reuven and Archik. A robust peasant with a ready smile, Katarina had been with the rabbi and rebbetzin for many years. With the exception of local officials, Katarina had never seen non-Jews visit the rabbi.

"Who are these two?" she asked.

"My helpers," Menachem Mendel answered offhandedly. Fortunately, the rebbetzin then entered and no further explanation was necessary.

The rebbetzin smiled a warm greeting to her Shabbos guest. "Reb Menachem Mendel," she exclaimed, "have you had any luck in replacing Vanka?"

A shrug and a sigh answered her question.

She then nodded towards the two *shkutzim* with him. "I'm sure Katarina can put up your two helpers over Shabbos," she said. She was about to call her servant when something in Menachem Mendel's expression stopped her. He leaned closer and briefly whispered their story, making it clear that for the boys' protection it was best not to alert anyone to their true identity.

With a sharp look at the peddler, the rebbetzin called to Katarina to head home, assuring her that she could finish up herself. She then seated Archik and Reuven at her large, wooden table and poured them tea from a lovely samovar.

Minutes after Katarina's departure, the rabbi joined them. As he entered the room, Menachem Mendel lifted his broad bulk off the bench, smiled broadly, and embraced his old friend.

"*Vus macht a Yid*, Reb Menachem Mendel?" Before his guest could reply, Rabbi Chaim Leib Kimelblat's mouth dropped open at the sight of the two *shkutzim* seated at his table. He tugged nervously at his curly, black beard, waiting for an explanation.

It was the rebbetzin who came forward and repeated Menachem Mendel's tale.

Rabbi Kimelblat shook his head, his eyes pools of sadness. "Oy," he groaned, "look to what lengths our children must go to save their lives!" He could not take his eyes off them. It was as if he were looking at children who had been resurrected from the dead.

Sipping tea, a sugar cube held between his teeth, the rabbi questioned the boys. "How did you escape from the canton?" he probed. "And how did you elude capture all these months?" Archik wiped the cake crumbs from his chin with a white, linen napkin and began to recount their escape and their recent encounters with bandits and cossacks. He spoke of the reward that had been posted for them, and of their fears that Kolchak was still on their trail. Reuven then added in a deep voice, "Without the help of the *Ribono shel olam,* we would not be here today. It is *HaKadosh Baruch Hu* who has kept us from the lion's mouth."

"Yes, my *teireh kinder*," the rabbi agreed, shaking his head, "it was truly the hand of God lifting you from the den of those murdering cossacks."

The rebbetzin had been standing by, her hands folded sedately before her, her eyes revealing her pain. "Rabbi," she said at last, "let the boys bathe before Shabbos." She cast a motherly eye their way. "Do you think Duvid's clothing will fit them?" she asked.

The rabbi smiled and returned her nod.

"And don't worry," the rebbetzin assured them, "I will see to it that your own clothing will be fresh and clean for your journey."

"Thank you so much for your kindness and hospitality," Reuven replied. And then, avoiding the rabbi's gaze, he swallowed hard and muttered, "Rabbi, please forgive my asking, but we are fearful of *khappers* and informers, and..." his voice trailed off.

The rabbi frowned. "I can well understand your anxiety, but you have nothing to fear in this village. We have never engaged *khappers*, nor shall we ever stoop to such dreadful means to fill the Czar's quotas, however painful it may be for us. Heaven forfend such a thought!" He smiled at them and his careworn face seemed to light up. "We have no *orchim* this Shabbos, and our children are all either married or in yeshivah. We are proud to have you with us." Reuven and Archik could not believe their good fortune. What a Shabbos it promised to be!

That evening after shul, dressed in the clean, white shirts and well-pressed, black trousers that belonged to the Kimelblats' youngest son, Duvid, they sat around a Shabbos table loaded with scrumptious food, listening eagerly to the words of Torah and joining in the zestful singing of *zemiros*. They shared the rabbi's joy when he announced, his eyes gleaming, "Tonight we can *bentch* with a *mezuman*."

Later, slipping between the sweet-smelling sheets, Reuven sighed, "Can you believe this is happening to us?"

There was no reply. Archik had fallen into a deep sleep.

Reuven shut his eyes and a passage from Tehillim suddenly came to mind:

> I will praise You, Hashem, with all my heart; I will recount Your marvelous acts. I will rejoice and exult in You; I will praise Your name, O Most High. When my enemies turn back, they stumble and perish before You. For You have upheld my judgment and my cause.... Hashem will be a stronghold for the oppressed, a stronghold in times of trouble. They who know Your name shall trust in You; for You, Hashem, do not forsake those who seek You.

The morning greeted Reuven and Archik with a chilling drizzle. After davening in the freezing synagogue, they were grateful for the rebbetzin's rich, steaming cholent. Rabbi Kimelblat apologized to the boys for not introducing them to his congregants. Of course he had planned to do so, he explained, but the weather had been so foul that before he could capture the congregation's attention, everyone had hastened home to his warm hearth.

"But rest assured, my dear boys, before the day is out, everyone will share our joy in knowing that our village hosted two courageous and faithful Jews this Shabbos."

Archik remarked that in shul they had been greeted

by curious and not particularly cordial stares.

"The *gabbai* never seemed to take his eyes off us," Reuven added with a shiver. "His expression wasn't friendly, either."

"But of course," the rabbi suddenly realized with dismay, "they saw you yesterday dressed in peasant clothing and today you were seated in our synagogue like good Jewish children davening! You must forgive me. I had completely forgotten how you two looked when you came into our village. No wonder they all stared—they didn't know what to make of you."

That afternoon, the village was to enjoy a special treat: a *derashah* by Reb Shaya the *gabbai*, who was known as a fiery orator. Despite the pouring rain, the synagogue was packed. Young and old alike elbowed their way toward the *bimah*, attempting to get as close as possible to the guest speaker.

Reb Shaya was a mountain of a man, and he carried himself with an air of self-importance. Pulling at his flowing beard, he waited with growing impatience for the congregation to grow still. When he finally rose, a hush fell over the boisterous throng. He towered over them. He paced the *bimah* in a slow, ponderous manner, and then turned sharply to scrutinize each and every face, his dark, brooding eyes boring deep into every heart. At last his gaze fell on the young, fresh faces of Reuven and Archik.

Rabbi Kimelblat rose to say a few words about his two Shabbos guests, but the *gabbai*, assuming the rabbi meant to introduce him, raised his hand to indicate that there was no need. He then began his stirring oration. A preacher of morals and virtue, Reb Shaya unleashed most of his fury on the two guests. He had seen Archik and Reuven enter the village dressed first as peasants, and then as Jewish children davening in the synagogue. He had also overheard the tale of two Jewish boys, dressed as *goyim*, rafting down the river, and deduced that they were simply runaways looking for adventure. All his righteous indignation, wrath, and censure were now directed at them.

Rabbi Kimelblat winced and tried to catch the *gabbai*'s attention, but with no success. He cleared his throat noisily, venturing less than discreet signals to Reb Shaya to stop the onslaught against two guiltless children. But caught up in his oratory, the *gabbai* continued his tirade against wayward boys who'd left their homes to go drifting about on a raft, dressing and acting like *shkutzim* and disgracing their parents with their disrespect for all things Jewish. It was just part and parcel of the degeneracy of the times, he concluded.

All eyes were fixed on Reuven and Archik, whose cheeks burned crimson. No longer able to contain himself, Rabbi Kimelblat overcame his reticence and placed a restraining arm on the *gabbai*.

"Forgive me for interrupting your sermon, Reb Shaya, but I must intervene before greater harm is done to two innocent children. I confess to my oversight. My failure to introduce my Shabbos guests to the congregation last night has led you to misconstrue their true nature."

The *gabbai* flushed and stared in astonishment as the rabbi motioned for Reuven and Archik to approach the *bimah*.

"Nothing I can say can do justice to the nobility of our Shabbos guests, Aharon Leib Gottlieb and Reuven Fenster, who have suffered the tortures of *Gehinnom* to remain faithful and loyal Jews. I beg my guests' *mechillah* for causing them so much pain, and I ask Reuven Fenster to tell you in his own words the true meaning of *mesiras nefesh*."

Painfully shy, Reuven turned pale and clasped his hands together to still their shaking. Gazing at all the faces looking up at him, he passed the back of his hand across his brow.

The rabbi took Reuven's hands in his own.

"My child, only you and Aharon Leib can express how young conscripts have suffered to remain Jews. I beg you, for the sake of all of us, describe everything. We must know the truth, no matter how painful."

Reuven took a deep breath and closed his eyes. Suddenly the words came gushing out like a river through a broken dam.

He spoke of his friendship with Archik, their flight, and their miraculous escape from death. He chronicled his first days as a conscript, the brutality of the cantons, the tortures and starvation and threat of baptism. He spared his listeners nothing: neither the beatings nor the death marches through snow and winter gales, and always the shadow of the cross, with vicious priests ready to capture a faltering soul.

Reuven mopped the tears from his eyes. Not a sound could be heard as the rain beat its mournful tap on the corrugated tin roof.

Reb Shaya's florid face had grown ashen. He solemnly walked over to Reuven and motioned for Archik to join them. "Today I judged you based on hearsay and gossip," he said in almost a whisper. "I beg you to forgive me for my *aveirah*. I have learned a painful lesson today, a lesson I shall take to heart and never forget."

Chapter 14

WHEN PLANNING THEIR latest outrage, Shmuel Shlagger, Yonah Kloptschik, and Velvel Shmuckler had faced only one problem. The horror of their scheme had presented no difficulty to men who hired themselves out as *khappers* to desperate *kehillos*, men who would grab a son from the arms of his grieving, widowed mother. No, there was another problem to overcome: They could easily steal a *sefer Torah*, but what respectable Jew would buy it from them? Who would be naive enough to deal with three known scoundrels?

It was Velvel who came up with the idea. They would use an intermediary, a man who was as much a *gonif* as they were, but not as well known: Kalman Fleishhocker, Shmuel Shlagger's brother-in-law, a man who operated on the edge of the law, and whose sincere manner had made him a successful swindler. This smooth talker would simply claim to be representing a family in such dire financial straits that they were forced to sell the *sefer Torah* that had been theirs for generations.

The *kehillah* of Salakas eagerly accepted Fleishhocker's tale of woe. The burglary had been easy, and now the beautiful Torah, cloaked in blue velvet and crowned with magnificent silver *rimonim*, was in the hands of the four rogues. Fleishhocker had found the perfect place to hide their ill-gotten treasure until it was to be delivered: A ferryboat had run aground and now rested in the shallows near the riverbank. No safer, more secluded hiding place could be found, he assured his cronies.

Reuven and Archik recited the *Shema*, wrapped themselves in their blankets against the occasional icy gust, and turned in for a peaceful night's sleep. The weather had been almost pleasant, with the wintry winds tempered by the sun's pastel rays, and according to the map they were just days away from Lithuania. Hopefully, the fall weather would not give way to an early winter blizzard, making an overland trek virtually impossible.

For now, they rafted on an unexpectedly calm river, as moonlight traced the inky water through a thickening layer of nimbus clouds.

Suddenly Archik gave a loud cry and pointed toward a huge, shadowy hulk near the shore. "Reuven, do you see what I see?"

Reuven's mouth dropped open. "It looks like a ghost ship!" he whispered.

"You have some imagination, Reuven," Archik chortled. "I bet it's just an abandoned ferry. The owners are probably waiting for the tide to shift before they float it off."

"I can always count on you to take the mystery out of life," Reuven grumbled.

"Well, if you really want mystery, what do you say we board the boat and take a look around?"

"Do you think it's safe?"

Archik shrugged. "Why not? Who would be prowling about on an abandoned ferry at this hour?"

"But what if the boat capsizes?"

Archik scratched his chin. "I think it's too low in the water for that. It's probably resting on the bottom. So should we chance it?"

The adventure was too enticing to resist. Reuven nodded his agreement.

The ferry loomed up out of the night like a slumbering leviathan. As they drew closer, Reuven spied a rope ladder dangling from the main deck, undoubtedly used by the escaping crew. They tied the raft to a mooring hook jutting out of the ferry's side and climbed the swaying ladder.

On deck they lit their lantern and began exploring. In the lantern's ghostly glow, the empty decks looked eerie. They entered a nearby cabin, where shawls, bundles of food, clothing, and dolls were scattered about. Clearly, the passengers had fled the sinking ferry in great haste.

The boys continued down the deck, whispering as if

afraid to awaken sleeping ghosts.

"Let's find the bridge," Archik said. "I've always wanted to steer a ship!"

They climbed up the companionway to the uppermost deck. Just as they reached the starboard cabins they halted in their tracks. Ahead, light poured out of a porthole.

"I think we have company," Reuven muttered under his breath.

"And I think we'd better leave."

Reuven put a finger to his lips, extinguished the lantern, and motioned for Archik to follow him. Crouching, the two made their way toward the light and peered through the porthole. Four tough-looking men stood staring down at a *sefer Torah* that lay open on what must have been the captain's chart table. Next to the *sefer* lay a blue velvet mantle with gold embroidery, casually discarded on the tabletop.

Reuven and Archik remained frozen in place, too startled to move.

A man with a deep scar running from his eye down his cheek suddenly turned toward the porthole.

"I keep feeling we're being watched," he grumbled.

The others waved away his fears.

"Who in the world could be watching us, Shmulik?" one of them growled. "Let's get back to business. I say the split's got to be even. I take the same risk you guys take."

The corners of Shmulik's mouth turned down into a sullen expression. "I say we took the greatest risk. We're the ones who stole it. Besides, it's our plan."

He looked again toward the porthole. "I still have the feeling someone's out there."

One of the men handed Shmulik a lantern. "Go look then," he said, exasperated. "We got to finish this business tonight. If we wait too long, the *kehillah* will hire a scribe. Then where will we all be?"

The boys scrambled away, their hearts pounding. They had just turned around the bend when they saw a beam of light flicker across the deck. They scurried down the companionway as noiselessly as they could. By the time they reached the rope ladder, their fear of being caught by these obviously ruthless men caught up with them. Reuven slipped several times, and the usually agile Archik lost his footing. For several long minutes he dangled precariously over the side of the ladder as Reuven, standing on the raft, tried to catch hold of him. At last he maneuvered the raft forward and grabbed Archik's foot, and Archik slithered down to safety.

Wasting no time, they cut the rope and began paddling furiously. Only when they were well away from the boat—and certain they could not be seen—did their pace slacken.

"Phew, that was a close call!" Archik said, letting out a huge wheeze as he broke the tense silence. "And thanks for keeping me dry," he grinned. "I wasn't in the mood for an icy bath."

Reuven managed a half-hearted smile in reply. He said nothing for some time and when he finally spoke, his tone could not conceal his outrage. "How could Jews steal a *sefer Torah*?"

Archik placed his hand on Reuven's hunched shoulder. "Reuven, you know that within all of us is a *yetzer hara* and a *yetzer hatov*. We all have the chance to choose the right way or the wrong way. You and I have learned that lesson the hard way. We have seen the best and worst in man. Why do some men choose evil? I'm not old enough or wise enough to answer that."

Reuven nodded. "I remember hearing my parents talk about someone in our village who was a thief. Surrounded by poverty, the thief lived well: his house was big, his children were well dressed, and his family never lacked food. His wife even marched about like a grand lady, dressed in the latest fashions and wearing a wig of human hair. So, my mother asked my father, where is justice? Why do the good suffer and the evil prosper? My father answered that it is only an illusion that the evil prosper. One cannot know their nightmares; their fear of retribution; their need to continually be on guard and survive in their base profession. He said that in God's good time, when it is their turn to face their Maker, justice will be done and their punishment will be meted out."

"But meanwhile, Reuven, we can't sit back and let those thieves get away with their plans. We've got to stop them!"

Reuven closed his eyes and swayed to and fro in thought. "We certainly can't go to the police," he said. We don't even know how they intend to sell the *sefer Torah* or where they stole it from."

"Well, we'll keep our eyes and ears open," Archik replied.

With that, the two dropped off into uneasy sleep.

One week later, Archik consulted his map carefully, then turned to Reuven. "This is it!" he cried, his eyes bright. "Get on your walking shoes—it's time to leave the river!"

They pulled their faithful raft ashore for the very last time at the outskirts of the town of Zarasai. Yet for some inexplicable reason, they once again concealed it among branches, twigs, and leaves as they had so many times in the past. The little craft had taken them so many miles; together they had survived raging rapids, summer squalls, and tempests, keeping afloat throughout their long and treacherous journey. Brushing the leaves from himself, Reuven muttered with a touch of melancholy, "Maybe some other boys in need of refuge will find our raft and it will take them to a safe harbor."

With their map and compass to guide them, they began their trek. According to Archik's calculations, they had a good 150-mile hike ahead of them. That meant they would reach their destination in a little over two weeks.

The day they set out, however, the weather turned foul, and a low, steel-gray sky warned of snow. They marched briskly, hugging themselves against the icy blasts. They could only hope to reach the town of Salakas before Shabbos, or they would spend yet another bitter day outdoors.

Sleet pelted them, biting into their faces. Through thickening fog and icy rain they heard the dull tolling of a church bell, a somber reminder of black-robed, Russian Orthodox priests, gleaming crucifixes, and the promise of pogroms.

They stomped past a scattering of cottages and huts. Yowling dogs could be heard over the wind as dusk moved quickly across the landscape. They continued walking, and camped only when they couldn't take another step. With fingers stiff from cold, they somehow managed to build a good fire. They snuggled close to the flames, wrapped in their fraying blankets.

Despite the miserable weather, they arrived in Salakas late Thursday night, with the wind howling and whipping their bodies and faces. For the moment they were grateful for the freezing, black night, which kept the townspeople in their homes. At the very least they could avoid the uproar that their appearance had caused in Druja.

They trudged through the empty streets, searching for signs of Jewish houses and a synagogue. Peering down an alley, a tall structure caught their eye. They had indeed located the town's impressive synagogue, much larger than the shuls they had seen recently. Noting a *mezuzah* on a doorpost, they knocked on the door nearest to the shul. A faint light flickering through the shuttered windows assured them that someone was still awake. Stamping the ground and pounding their hands together to keep from freezing, they waited impatiently for someone to answer their tapping.

Finally an old man, stooped with age, opened the door a crack. His teeth chattering from the cold, Reuven apologetically asked where they could find the town rabbi. "I am the rabbi," the man announced. "And what is it you want at this late hour?"

"*Mir zeinen Yidden*," Reuven muttered, introducing himself and his friend and briefly explaining their plight.

Overwhelmed at the sight of the two lads dressed as *shkutzim*, the astounded rabbi ushered them inside. Before another word was exchanged, the rabbi produced a basin of warm water, sweet-smelling soap, and fresh towels. Seated at last before a large fireplace with its well-stoked fire, they sipped tea eagerly. The rabbi had found his wife's freshly baked mandelbroit, and the lads sank their teeth into its luscious, crusty goodness.

Their host introduced himself as Rabbi Naphtali Ernstoff, the rabbi of the town of Salakas for the past fifty years. Once again, Reuven and Archik recounted their journey.

"And where are you boys heading?" the rabbi said, leaning forward, his hands steepled on the table.

Archik smiled wanly. "Toward Kovno. I have relatives there."

The rabbi rubbed a brow that resembled old parchment. He closed his eyes for a moment. "My dear children, you do know that here in Lithuania the Czar's heinous Cantonist Laws are in full force. The army has been hunting for Jewish runaways. If even a hint of your presence gets out you could be in grave danger." He paused thoughtfully. "Tell me, did anyone see you tonight?"

"We saw no one on the streets, Rabbi," Archik

answered.

"Good," Rabbi Ernstoff nodded. "Tomorrow morning, when you are dressed in proper Jewish clothing, I will introduce you as my great-nephews from Ternopol."

"But Rabbi, you may be endangering yourself. Perhaps someone did see us," Reuven declared gravely.

Rabbi Ernstoff's mouth curled into a smile and his eyes appeared to dance with laughter. "My dear boys, I am touched that you are concerned for my welfare. But rest assured," he said, holding up the palm of his hand, "at my age I fear no one, except for the *Ribono shel olam*. And He, blessed be His name, has dealt kindly with me all my years."

"Rabbi Naphtali, how can we ever thank you?" Archik exclaimed.

Once again the rabbi smiled. "Thank me? No, my child, I thank you and the *Ribono shel olam* for granting me an extraordinary mitzvah on a very special day. In honor of my fiftieth anniversary as the rabbi of Salakas, the *kehillah* has purchased a beautiful *sefer Torah* for our synagogue. Tomorrow I will have the privilege of standing under the *chuppah* and carrying the *sefer Torah* into our shul. So, my dear boys," he said smiling warmly, "you have chosen a fine day to visit the town of Salakas and its aging rabbi."

Reuven felt his mouth grow dry. He glanced at Archik uneasily. "Rabbi, do you by any chance know where the *kehillah* obtained the *sefer Torah*?"

His brow raised, the rabbi scrutinized his guests.

"From what I understand, it was purchased from an upstanding man, an *ehrlicheh Yid* whose family had come upon hard times and was forced to sell its beautiful Torah scroll, which had been in the family for generations. Why do you ask?"

In a trembling voice, Reuven recounted their recent adventure aboard the grounded ferry.

Rabbi Ernstoff rose, his face ashen. Pacing the floor, he pressed the boys for additional information about the *sefer Torah* and its thieves.

"You say the man you saw was stout. Surely there is no lack of corpulent people about," he pointed out, forcing a smile.

Reuven then described the *sefer Torah*, with its beautiful blue mantle embroidered with gold, and its exquisite, silver *rimonin*.

Rabbi Ernstoff stopped his pacing. "First thing tomorrow, we will call upon the *gabbai*, Reb Shalom Weisel. I want you to tell him exactly what you have told me. Then I want you to examine the *sefer Torah*. Before any accusation is made, we must be absolutely certain that this is the Torah you saw that night. If you are right, the festivities will be postponed and action will be taken."

No one slept well that night. Reuven tossed and turned. He knew that his revelation had caused Rabbi Ernstoff great anguish. And what if it was not the same *sefer Torah* after all? Perhaps he should have held his peace. Still, how could he have in good conscience withheld what he thought to be true? The *sefer Torah* had to be returned to its rightful owners.

They davened *shacharis* in the cold dawn and headed for the home of Reb Shalom Weisel, arriving as he was about to sit down to his morning meal. The rabbi came right to the point. He insisted that Reuven describe what he had seen on the ferry. As he did so, the stunned *gabbai*'s appetite evaporated.

Reb Shalom led them straight to the new *sefer Torah*, which was covered with a white shawl. Reb Weisel removed the shawl and both boys gasped. There it was, wrapped in its blue mantle. They were now more certain this was the very Torah they had seen in the hands of the four scoundrels.

The *gabbai* turned to the rabbi, mopping his brow with a white, linen handkerchief.

"I must admit something to you," he said feebly. "When I had the *sefer Torah* checked by Reb Chaim Romberg the *sofer*, he informed me that it seemed to have been written quite recently. Of course I was taken aback, since Reb Kalman Fleishhocker had insisted that the Torah had been with his family for generations."

"And why did you not mention this to me?" the rabbi said sharply.

"I was certain Reb Kalman had only wished to raise the price of the *sefer Torah* by giving it a more *yichusdikeh* history. I never imagined that so foul a deed had taken place," he confessed, obviously shaken.

The rabbi unrolled the *sefer Torah* and studied it for a moment, then motioned the boys closer. "You didn't see the scroll up close, I imagine."

They were about to say no when Archik gasped, his

hand raised to his mouth.

"What is it, my child?" the rabbi asked.

Archik spoke quietly. "Some months ago, Reuven and I had the *zechus* to write a letter in a *sefer Torah.* Because my name is Aharon Leib I wrote two letters, the *aleph* and *lamed* of the *sefer*'s last word. When I placed my hand over the *sofer*'s, it shook, and my letters came out slightly thicker than the others. I was upset by what I had done but the *sofer* assured me that as long as the lettering was clear, the *sefer Torah* was kosher. And those," he said, his entire body quivering, "those are my *aleph* and *lamed*."

That Sunday morning, a delegation left Salakas with the *sefer Torah* in tow. Rabbi Ernstoff had begged to join them, but due to his age, the *kehillah* had refused. They assured Reuven and Archik that as soon as the Torah was returned to its rightful owners, Fleishhocker and his gang would receive their just deserts. The *gabbai* hinted that all four would likely be placed in *cherem.*

One of the townspeople insisted on taking Archik and Reuven to Kovno in his wagon. "Just a small token of our town's gratitude for your vigilance," the man proclaimed.

Reuven and Archik could not believe their good fortune. Still, it was with a heavy heart that they parted from Rabbi Ernstoff.

"We are truly sorry for spoiling the festivities in your honor, Rabbi," Reuven said.

The rabbi's eyes shone with warmth. "My dear children, yours was an act of *chesed*," he told them, clapping them both on their backs. "It was the *Ribono shel olam* who guided you to our town in order to prevent a great transgression from taking place."

Climbing aboard the wagon, they waved farewell to the Jews of Salakas, who had already engaged Reb Chaim Romberg to write a *sefer Torah* in honor of their rabbi.

Chapter 15

REB SHIMON FEINHOLTZ of Salakas, the generous man who had volunteered to drive Reuven and Archik to Kovno, regaled the boys with tales of his own boyhood adventures, making the long, tedious trip bearable. As they approached Kovno, he suggested that his passengers change into their Jewish clothing. In his slow, ponderous way, Reb Shimon explained that in Kovno, *shkutzim* who later turned out to be Jews would draw undue attention to themselves. So Archik and Reuven concealed themselves behind a copse of shrubs and trees and rid themselves of their disguise once and for all.

Kovno was bathed in a winter twilight that painted its raw poverty in pastel colors. With some local assistance, they located the Ehrlichmans' home on the outskirts of the town's Jewish sector. It was a modest-sized, wooden structure with freshly painted, green shutters and a well-tended vegetable garden. Several geese and ducks waddled by and a cow ruminated in a barn at the rear of the house.

Yet the bucolic tranquility did not soothe Archik's emotions. He stared at the door for what seemed to Reuven an inordinately long time, and when he finally tapped lightly, beads of perspiration speckled his brow.

The door was opened by a balding man wearing a high, black yarmulke. Laugh lines were etched deep in the corners of his eyes, and his ruddy cheeks were framed by a soft, curly, graying beard. He squinted in the twilight at the two travel-weary lads.

"Uncle Misha?"

The man started, peering without recognition at the young man before him.

"I am your nephew, Aharon Leib," he stammered.

The man gripped the doorpost and the color drained from his face. "Fanya, Fanya, come quickly!" he shouted.

Anticipating the worst, Fanya Ehrlichman was at her husband's side in seconds. "Fanya," Misha managed to find his voice, "our Archikel is here!"

The reunion was heartrending; Misha and Fanya could not contain their tears of joy. Although their Archikel was a bit thin, he was as handsome as they could have ever imagined. The following day, after the boys were well fed and well rested, Misha Ehrlichman turned to his wife with a glimmer in his eye. "The tears that flowed in our home yesterday could have filled a reservoir!" he teased.

Misha was a good-humored man, and both Archik and Reuven took to him right away. After a hearty afternoon meal around a massive, oak dining room table, Reuven and Archik asked if they could safely write their parents.

Misha shook his head dourly. "Not just yet, boys," he said. "We must be careful. One can never know who might trace such letters. But the moment we are certain it is safe to do so, your parents will share in the knowledge that you are safe and well. If it makes you feel better," he added cheerfully, "I will give you paper and you may write your letters now. We'll send them when the time is right."

In spare, simple sentences, Reuven assured his parents that, *baruch Hashem*, he was in good health, and that despite all his difficulties he had remained a faithful Jew. He prayed that they, too, were healthy, and promised that one day, when the terrible Cantonist Laws were annulled, he would be reunited with them. It had been years since Reuven had thought so intently about his home and his family, and it took all his resolve not to break down in a flood of tears.

Later that day, Archik confided to his friend that his aunt and uncle seemed to feel guilty about having given him away rather than bringing him up themselves. "I just want them to know that I have the most wonderful momma and poppa in the world, and the best sisters," he declared. "I don't want them to apologize to me."

Reuven understood his feelings and agreed that he should make them known as soon as possible.

The opportunity presented itself as they were seated around the hearth after dinner. Archik directed the conversation towards his adoptive family, describing them with great warmth and love. But instead of reassuring them, his words impelled them to explain why they had given him up and how painful it had been for them.

"In the few months you were with us, we grew to love you as if you were our own child. The moment I handed you over to Penina, my heart broke," Fanya confided. "You cannot know how difficult it was for us. And when we received the letter from Avrum telling us that his beloved Archik had been kidnapped and conscripted into the Czar's army...." Her next words were strangled in sobs.

Misha blew his nose noisily and mopped his eyes with a huge handkerchief. Taking a deep breath, he continued where Fanya left off. "You see, my boy, though we had come to love you as our own, we did not feel competent to care for a baby at our advanced stage in life. And we had already made a commitment to our friend Gershom Lader to use our home as a safe haven for cantonist runaways. Under such circumstances, the presence of an infant would have been dangerous for all."

Reuven looked at Uncle Misha, startled. "Did you say your friend's name was Gershom Lader?"

Misha nodded. "Why, do you know Reb Gershom?"

"Yes. It was he who raised the ransom to save us from the bandits," Reuven said.

There was a moment of stunned silence.

"*Guttenyu*!" Fanya finally sputtered, her eyes wide with astonishment. "Reb Gershom told us the terrible story! We had no idea that he had rescued our very own Archikel and his friend...."

The days that followed were dreamlike. Reuven and Archik were treated like visiting dignitaries, with Tante Fanya fussing over them and plying them with delicacies.

With the approach of Shabbos, Archik once again took Reuven aside and divulged his inner turmoil.

"Reuven, I know I am being a coward for not telling Uncle Misha and Tante Fanya my real reason for coming here. But I keep thinking how terrible they'll feel when they learn that I've come to discover the truth about my real parents. Believe me, Reuven, it's not that I don't love my adoptive parents. In my heart, they will always be momma and poppa to me. But inside, something keeps pushing me to find out whether, by some miracle, my real mother and father are still alive. Maybe I even have sisters and brothers," he said, biting his lip to still his emotions as he slumped dejectedly in his seat. "I know it sounds insane, but I think my real parents are alive and mourning for me. What should I do, Reuven?" he moaned. "I don't want to hurt Tante Fanya and Uncle Misha, but I have to tell them the truth."

His head bowed, Reuven rubbed his cheek with his index finger. He *had* wondered why Archik had avoided telling his relatives the reason for their escaping to Lithuania, of all places, where the Cantonist Laws were in full force. What puzzled him even more was why the

Ehrlichmans hadn't asked why they had made their way to Lithuania instead of the safety of Latvia. Perhaps they knew the reason but preferred to ignore it for the time being.

He turned to Archik. "Look, there is no great rush," he said thoughtfully. "We don't have to burst their bubble during the first week. Besides, sometimes things have a way of working themselves out. You'll see. One day you will find a way to steer the conversation onto the subject of how your uncle found you, and then, in an offhand way, you'll say that you have always been curious about your parents and would like to find out about them."

Reuven's counsel was soothing, and Archik bided his time.

From the very first day, the Ehrlichmans had warned the two boys to stay out of sight. "Even in Lithuania, I am sorry to admit, we have *khappers* and informers, not to mention the police and the army," Misha remarked. "We know the situation here very well, my lads. After all, for the past sixteen years our home has been a way station for runaways."

"Until the right palms have been greased it is best to keep a low profile," Fanya agreed.

Following this advice was particularly difficult that first Shabbos, however. Reuven and Archik gazed longingly at Misha Ehrlichman, bedecked in his finest Shabbos caftan, headed for shul. Instead of accompanying him, they had to once again daven without a *minyan*, secluded in the Ehrlichmans' home. Seeing their pained expressions, Fanya assured them that it was only a matter of time before they could leave the house. But for the present, she counseled patience.

Some of their disappointment was erased by the delicious Shabbos meals Tante Fanya served: boiled carp, bowls of chicken soup rich in homemade egg noodles, roast chicken and oven-browned potatoes, a superb compote, glasses of tea, and feather-light sponge cake. Though stuffed, everyone managed to join in the rousing *zemiros*, which culminated in a joyous and deeply felt recitation of *birkas hamazon*. Misha closed his eyes as he leaned back in his chair, his face radiant with contentment.

"Uncle Misha, how did your home happen to become a hiding place for runaway cantonists?" Archik asked, breaking into the man's reverie.

Misha launched into his reply with relish. "Just when all our children were married and out of the house, and we were looking forward to quietly enjoying our grandchildren, our old friend Gershom Lader came along and changed our retirement plans," he said with a chuckle.

"He asked us to take upon ourselves the great mitzvah of saving Jewish lives. How could we refuse such a call?" Fanya added.

"Once we agreed to this role, our friend assured us he would take care of the heavy bribes needed to keep enemies from our door," Misha continued.

"By the way, we have a wonderful surprise for you. Reb Gershom has just returned to Lithuania. After a visit to his relatives in Vilna, he will spend next Shabbos with us."

Leaning over, he placed his hand on Archik's shoulder. "And then you can thank him personally for saving your lives."

The week passed in a haze of contentment, with plenty to eat, plenty of freedom to observe mitzvos and even read a bit from Uncle Misha's small library of *sefarim*, and enough motherly care from Tante Fanya to satisfy two boys who'd been on their own much too long.

Gershom Lader's arrival on Friday was an additional reason for celebration. The boys immediately took to the tall, rugged-faced man who had saved them from a terrible death. Archik was particularly smitten.

"He's everything I wish I could be," Archik confided to his friend that night after a superlative dinner.

Reuven agreed sleepily.

"He has adventures, and takes risks, and faces danger all the time. And yet, he is so quiet, so ready to hear others talk. You know," Archik said thoughtfully, "maybe Gershom is the one I should talk to about finding my real parents. After all, he knows my aunt and uncle intimately. Perhaps he can help me broach the subject."

After Shabbos, when Gershom was packing up his wagon and preparing to go, Archik finally found the courage to bring up the topic.

"Reb Gershom," he began hesitantly, "perhaps you can help me."

"What is it, Archik?" Gershom turned a kindly eye upon the boy. He was a fine lad, he and his companion, brave and good-hearted. It was not often that Gershom got to see the fruit of his efforts; this was true *nachas*.

Archik's words broke into his reverie. "I was adopted as an infant, you see, and I want to find out what happened to my natural parents, but I'm not sure how to go about it."

Gershom's eyebrows lifted. Whatever request he'd expected, it had surely not been this.

"Tell me more, Archik."

Archik once more repeated the story he'd told Reuven. Lost in his own emotions, he hardly noticed Gershom's increasing agitation.

"Please forgive me for taking up your time with my personal concerns," Archik ended. "I don't know why I even troubled you with my nonsense."

Gershom studied the boy's face as one would study a map.

"Archik, don't apologize," he said, placing his hand on the lad's arm. "Your desire isn't nonsense, it's sensible and serious—more serious than you may understand. Tell me, do you happen to have the note you spoke of, the note the gypsies gave your uncle?"

Archik drew out a small, leather pouch he always wore about his waist, and handed Gershom the yellowed, crumpled paper. Gershom blinked several times as he scrutinized the fine, feminine handwriting.

"May I take this with me? It is quite important, I assure you."

Puzzled, Archik reluctantly agreed.

Leaving his cart only half-loaded, Gershom returned to the dining room to study the note. He could hardly contain his excitement as he read the scrawled plea. The pieces of the puzzle were finally coming together, but there were still several points to be cleared up with Misha. He had to be absolutely certain before he took the final step.

He called to his host and hostess, who were busily cleaning up in the kitchen. His somber tone made Misha and Fanya apprehensive. As he repeated his conversation with Archik, their expressions revealed their distress.

"But he told us that he loved Avrum and Penina as if they were his own parents," Fanya contended, her voice charged with anger. "He even assured us they were the best parents in the world. And now you tell me that he is still yearning to find his real parents? Such disloyalty!" she fumed. "I can't believe such a thing. How could he? And worse, he tells all this to you, a complete stranger!"

"Fanya, I beg you, calm yourself. He came to me because he sensed you would misunderstand and be hurt. And now I see that he was right. Try to appreciate the child's natural desire to find his parents, which in no way diminishes his devotion to your niece and nephew. He is a child and his feelings are normal. He wants to find out where he comes from. He wonders whether his real parents are still alive. Is that so unnatural? Try to understand, and don't judge the boy harshly."

Slowly, both Fanya and Misha composed themselves. Gershom then asked Misha to recollect when and where he had discovered the child and the details of his search for the parents. When all his doubts had been laid to rest, Gershom shared with them a tale of pathos and pain;

of a mother brutally murdered in a pogrom; of a father seriously injured and wandering from village to village in search of his lost infant son; of a man who, in his despair, plunged into business and ultimately built a fortune and rebuilt a life.

He then revealed to the astonished couple the name of the man who'd experienced the tragedy—the man who was Archik's father.

Chapter 16

"WELL, YOU *ARE* a man of surprises," the Baron told his friend as the two sat together in his richly appointed study. "What in the world brings you to England?"

Gershom Lader shifted uncomfortably in his chair. He had planned this conversation over and over on the stormy boat trip, but somehow all of his words suddenly seemed pat and meaningless. How do you tell a man that you have found the son he lost fifteen years before?

"Itzik, do you remember the last time we met? When you so generously gave me the money to ransom two boys?"

The Baron waved his hand. "It was not generosity, Gershom. It was my obligation."

"Whatever the case, I've since met the two lads, Aharon Leib Gottlieb and Reuven Fenster. They are good boys, Itzik, courageous and faithful to Hashem. Boys any father would be proud of."

The Baron looked shrewdly at Gershom. He knew his old friend had not traveled such a long distance just to flatter him or waste time in idle chatter.

"I'm glad to hear they are well," Baron Rothenberg said quietly.

Gershom rubbed a hand over his wet brow. Winter in England, and he was sweating!

"Itzik," he began again, "Hashem works in incredible, wonderful ways. He rewards *tzedakah* a hundredfold."

A life spent in business dealings had long since taught Baron Isaac Anshel Rothenberg how to be patient. Still, he was curious about Gershom's visit and his uncharacteristic difficulty in getting to the point.

"Gershom, what exactly are you trying to tell me?"

He took a deep breath. "Itzik, I have reason to believe that Archik Gottlieb is your lost son."

The Baron paled, stood up from his chair, then fell back down onto it. He spoke in a voice choked with emotion, a voice that hardly sounded like his own.

"My...my son? Gershom, what are you saying?" Wordlessly, Gershom handed the Baron Archik's note. He read it and reread it, the tears coursing down his cheeks. "My son! A miracle, Gershom, a miracle!"

"What shall I say to him?" Itzik muttered as the two headed for Kovno, their hastily arranged sea voyage behind them.

Gershom Lader chuckled. "The words will come to you when you see him, believe me."

"You say he looks like my Sarah?"

"The image."

The Baron shook his head in disbelief. "It is like a dream, a dream."

They arrived at the Ehrlichmans' late Thursday. Fanya gaped at her illustrious guest, unable to utter more than a few hoarse words of welcome. At last, when everyone was seated around the dining room table, sipping brandy, all the pieces of the puzzle were put together.

"I have no way of repaying you for rescuing my son," the Baron said with deep emotion.

"I played but a small role, I must admit," Misha Ehrlichman said. "The real credit goes to my niece and nephew, Penina and Avrum Gottlieb. They are the ones who loved and reared the boy as their own."

Baron Rothenberg rubbed his forehead. "I shall always be indebted to all of you."

"Shall I call Archik?" Fanya asked.

The Baron took a deep breath. "Yes, bring in my son."

When Archik entered, he knew that something unusual was in the air. He gazed from face to face, his eyes coming to rest on the stranger in the room. He had not been told that he would be meeting his father for fear of an "*ayin hara*," as Fanya had insisted, though she had hinted to him that he was in for a wondrous piece of news. The stranger rose and Archik sent searching glances to his uncle and aunt, and then to Gershom Lader.

"Aharon Leib," the Baron said softly, "my name is Yitzchak Rothenberg."

Archik cocked his head. "Are you Baron Rothenberg, sir? The man who gave the ransom money for us?"

The Baron smiled.

Archik extended his hand. "Sir, I want to thank you." He then turned to his uncle. "Uncle Misha, I know that Reuven would like to thank the Baron, too. Should I call him in?"

"Later, Archikel," his uncle replied with an enigmatic smile.

"Aharon Leib," the Baron continued, "I understand you came all the way to Lithuania in the hope of discovering news of your family?"

"Yes, I did. Did you know my family, sir?"

The Baron's voice wavered with emotion. "Your mother was an *eishes chayil*, Archik. And I..." his voice broke.

Archik stared at him for a long moment. "My father," he whispered.

Before either could say another word, they fell into each other's arms.

Needless to say, there was not a dry eye in the room.

Chapter 17

Cheshvan 1845

My very dear friend Reuven,

How can I describe my life here in England? No fairy tale could have a happier ending. My father is the kindest and most generous man in the world and he is very eager to do everything he can to please me. My gentle stepmother has accepted me into her home as if I were her very own. My sisters are also very kind to me; in fact, behind my parents' backs, they constantly ply me with the most delicious chocolates. They insist that I am pale and undernourished, although I assure them that I am hale and hearty. I fear that all this pampering will turn me into an overindulged dandy.

My new home is like a palace. I just cannot find the

words to describe it. We have acres and acres of lawns, woods, and even our own lake. My own room is at the top of a huge spiral staircase. I sleep in an oversized bed—a far cry from the hard ground of Russia—and a valet lays out my clothing and is always at my beck and call. I know this all sounds incredible, but believe me, it's true.

And now to business. I cannot stay here living the life of the idle rich and eating chocolate bonbons all day. (Imagine my rejecting such an idea a year ago!) I've been studying English with a tutor, but that can't really fill my life. I've decided, and my father agrees, that what I need now is the Torah learning that circumstances never allowed me. I hope to study with a rebbe here at home for a while, making up for lost time, and then, if the Cantonist Laws are ever revoked, perhaps I can travel back to Lithuania and study in a yeshivah there.

And where do you come in, my old friend? You can't stay in Kovno forever, though my aunt and uncle would surely love you to! Lithuania is still a dangerous spot for you, and even the Baron's influence might not help if the Czar's soldiers find you.

What I propose is this: Join me here in England. Together we can study, and maybe even find time for some adventures! Here you will be safe, and you can even correspond with your parents.

My father thinks it's a good idea—I suspect he wants you to keep me out of trouble. (I'm still the same Archik, you see!) I'm taking the liberty of enclosing your steamship ticket and some money for expenses. And don't be too proud to accept it, because I'm doing this as much for me as for you.

I have also invited my adoptive parents to visit with us this summer. My father has assured me that he will provide handsome dowries for my adoptive sisters, and that my good family, who so lovingly cared for me, will never know need again. As I said, my father is a wonderful man, and as each day goes by, I learn more about how hard he struggles for the benefit of Klal Yisrael.

I look forward to seeing you shortly.

Your friend,
Archik

Reuven bid the Ehrlichmans a tearful goodbye and boarded the coach that would carry him to the port of Riga. He was to spend a week there before embarking on his voyage to England.

Riga was a teeming port city with a large and prosperous Jewish community. The Ehrlichmans had arranged for Reuven to stay with their old friend, Mordechai Drucker, a printer and publisher of *sefarim*. The Druckers were a warm family and Reuven was made to feel most welcome in their noisy household of ten boisterous children. Reb Mordechai even took him on a tour of the printing house, where he gawked at the huge presses and the hundreds of bound volumes.

It was an exhilarating week for the *shtetl* lad. For the first time in his life, Reuven found himself in a cosmopolitan setting. The house was spacious and well appointed, with comfortably overstuffed settees and velvet draperies adorning the long-faced windows.

The family was not wealthy, but from Reuven's limited perspective, he assumed that Archik's surroundings in England would be roughly the same.

Despite the recurrent cold drizzle, which often turned into a downpour, Reuven enjoyed strolling down the city's busy streets, darting between the horse-drawn carriages, and davening in Riga's lovely synagogue. He drank in the shul's splendor, his eyes bright.

One rare sunny day, he headed for the pier to admire the tall sailing ships. Mouth agape, he watched muscular men load and unload cargo, and he waved farewell to the vessels gliding out to sea and off to exotic ports. Seated on a wooden post amidst thick coils of hemp, he dreamed of far-off places like Siam, Japan, the South Sea Islands. What were they like?

He heaved a contented sigh. A world traveler he wasn't; England was far enough for him. Besides, he'd had enough adventure these past few years to last him a lifetime. No, he wanted to spend the rest of his life living as a Jew.

He turned his head—and the world came crashing in. There, just a few yards behind him, were four uniformed soldiers. Was it Kolchak still on his trail? Was it some other group of soldiers hunting for fugitives? Were they looking for him? Reuven jumped up from the post. His response was almost a reflex: it had not been that long since he'd faced those ominous uniforms. There was no panic, no fear, just the knowledge that he had to get away. Far away.

He bolted past a group of burly stewards, oblivious

to their angry curses. He heard men shouting in Russian: "Hey you! Stop! Now!" He ignored them, racing on.

He vaulted over several crates, scraping his knees on the endless rows of containers waiting to be hoisted aboard. He was soaked in his own sweat. Stopping to catch his breath, he glanced over his shoulder. With every passing moment, the soldiers drew closer.

He turned a corner. They would be onto him in a flash. Even if they hadn't been looking for him, surely his flight had aroused their suspicions—and capture meant certain death.

Suddenly Reuven noticed a crate lying forgotten in a corner. Without thinking he jumped into it and pulled the lid closed. It was dark inside, and moist and putrid, but it was safe.

Reuven dimly heard footsteps and shouts. Then the noise passed and all was silent. Afraid to peek out for even a moment, the boy sat in the closed atmosphere, hardly daring to breathe; his head spun.

After what seemed an eternity, he heard footsteps once again. Had the soldiers returned? He heard the sound of wood hitting the hard floor, felt his own refuge being carried up, up into darkness. His stomach turned, his head whirled. There was a great crash, and he heard no more.

Eventually, the strong, salty sea air seeping in through the slats of the crate woke him. He rubbed his eyes, confused. Where was he? Then he remembered: he was locked in a crate to escape the soldiers! Cautiously, Reuven prodded the lid open. His sore body protesting, he crawled out into the darkness.

When his eyes finally adjusted to the blackness, he saw hundreds of crates and barrels, one piled upon the other. Once again, Hashem had not forsaken him. By some miracle, the crate in which he had sought refuge had not been sandwiched beneath the others.

He tried to grope his way toward the hold's exit when a heavy sea roll caught him off balance and he was thrown to the ground. He rose unsteadily on rubbery legs. Reuven's stomach churned and he felt the bile rise in his throat. He just had to make his way out of the hold and into the fresh air. Finally, at the far end of the cavernous room, he saw a ladder. Struggling forward, he clambered out.

Reuven took a deep breath, his face whipped by sea spray and a blustery wind. The ship rolled in the heavy sea and he held his spinning head, yearning for a glass of tea to settle his stomach. He felt a hand on his shoulder and whirled about to find himself facing a strapping, bronzed sailor. The man pushed him forward, babbling in a harsh-sounding, foreign tongue, but a bewildered Reuven understood not a word.

In seconds he found himself in a small cabin lined with personal effects, a table, and a bunk bed. Seated behind the table was a formidable-looking man dressed in a captain's uniform. The man was short and beefy, with a thick, graying mustache which wove into his bushy sideburns. He clutched a briar pipe between his teeth as he sized up the boy.

"You don't look like the usual stowaway," he said in

English, his grin revealing a full set of white teeth. "And you don't understand a word I've said, do you, laddy?" He proceeded to repeat his remarks in very broken Russian.

Reuven wiped the tears that gathered unwillingly as he answered. "Sir, I am not a stowaway. I was running from some...bullies, and I hid in a crate."

"You are a Jew?"

Reuven swallowed hard and nodded yes. He then rummaged through his pockets and drew out his steamship ticket, which he handed to the captain.

The captain examined the ticket and shook his head sorrowfully. "So you were heading to England and traveling first class?"

Not quite understanding the implication of the captain's words, Reuven gaped at the man, his eyes wide with confusion.

"Now look here, young fellow, we are heading for America, with a stopover in Nova Scotia. We cannot detour to England. Do you understand?"

Yes, Reuven nodded once more, he most certainly did.

"Now, laddy, what is your name?"

"Reuven, sir, Reuven Fenster."

"Rubin, hear me out. I will see to it that you get suitable clothing for the duration of the journey. You will work as a cabin boy and assist my personal steward, John Dooley. Do your work well, follow orders, and keep to yourself, and I promise you a safe crossing. I can do no more for you. Do I make myself clear?"

Reuven shook his head ruefully. The captain summoned John Dooley, an Irishman with a craggy face that looked as if it had been crushed by a sledgehammer, and steel-gray eyes as piercing as a dagger. Reuven felt his knees buckle as he waited for the captain to issue orders to his steward. The man listened with one eye on his new charge.

Reuven reflected that he had best start learning this strange new language. John Dooley motioned for Reuven to follow. As they left the captain's cabin, Reuven hesitated for a second. He looked up at the shimmering stars that covered the sky like brilliant shards of glass. Inhaling the brisk sea air, he muttered a prayer of thanksgiving. *Baruch Hashem*, he was safe and away from Russia. Maybe, he reflected, the *Ribono shel olam* had plans for him in the New World.

He shrugged and whispered, "So let it be."